THE BLEEDS

THE BLEEDS

A Novel

DIMITRI NASRALLAH

ESPLANADE
Books

THE FICTION IMPRINT AT VÉHICULE PRESS

ESPLANADE BOOKS IS THE FICTION IMPRINT AT VÉHICULE PRESS

Published with the generous assistance of the Canada Council for the Arts, the Canada Book Fund of the Department of Canadian Heritage, and the Société de développement des entreprises culturelles du Québec (SODEC).

Editor : Andrew Steinmetz
Cover design: David Drummond
Photo of author: Roger Aziz
Typeset in Minion by studio oneonone
Printed by Marquis Printing Inc.

Library and Archives Canada Cataloguing in Publication

Nasrallah, Dimitri, 1978–, author
The bleeds / Dimitri Nasrallah.

Issued in print and electronic formats.
ISBN 978-1-55065-480-6 (softcover) –ISBN 978-1-55065-488-2 (EPUB)

I. Title.

PS8627.A78B54 2018   C813'.6   C2017-903132-5
C2017-903133-3

Published by Véhicule Press, Montréal, Québec, Canada
vehiculepress.com

Distribution in Canada by LitDistCo
www.litdistco.ca

Distribution in the U.S. by Independent Publishers Group
www.ipgbook.com

Printed in Canada on FSC certified paper.

for Niko Karaam

PART 1

CHOICES

THE NATION

MAHBAD'S NEWS SOURCE SINCE 1964

Violence Mars Vote

Four dead, 50 injured in referendum on Bleed rule

BY NADA FERBER

Pitched battles between voters and police left four people dead and nearly 50 injured across Qala Phratteh and its surrounding suburbs, as huge numbers flocked to the polls Tuesday to render judgment on President Vadim Bleed's first mandate.

When polls closed at 9 p.m., frustration boiled over with mobs overturning cars and burning tires to block off roads. The violence came after the government suspended balloting in several opposition-friendly districts to investigate claims of observer meddling.

Only a month ago, many assumed the election would be an easy exercise to crown the 37-year-old incumbent. But by the end of the day, Vadim Bleed, the third generation of his family to lead the country, is fighting for his political life.

Sensing the dynasty is at its most vulnerable after 50 years in power, the opposition New Nationalists Party called the election a referendum on the Bleed presidency.

NNP opposition leader Dabny Bolshoi has tried to tap into the frustrations of voters who have not loved Bleed as much as they did his grandfather, Blanco, nor respected him as they did his father, Mustafa.

The NNP has petitioned the United Nations for international observers to counter the corruption they say has plagued past votes. It's not a move that has pleased the Bleed government. "What the NNP calls international observers, we consider international interference," said Minister of the Interior Constantin Benini.

Polls opened at 9 a.m. to lineups that began forming at dawn, and by

9

midday in some towns they stretched for blocks. As lines outside polling stations grew longer, voter frustration turned to outright anger.

Observers have noted the higher-than-expected turnout reflected a desire for change. Across the country, from the Lezer heartlands in the northwest to the uranium-mining towns in the south and isolated villages throughout the Allegory Mountains, unemployment has spiked during the past five years, as has the cost of most basic goods.

Efforts to diversify the economy, a central promise of Bleed's first mandate, have either stagnated or failed to materialize. Meanwhile, relations between the Bleed government and the uranium-mining industry have fallen to an all-time low as the administration seeks increased royalties while threatening nationalization.

Bleed had been noticeably struggling in the final stretch of the campaign. Nowhere was this more apparent than at his final rally at Bleed Raceway, where the former Formula One champ delivered a speech to fewer than 2,000 supporters. The campaign cited strong winds and the threat of a thunderstorm for the event's poor attendance.

But if bad weather kept Bleed's supporters away, the poor turnout appeared to encourage the NNP. Its candidates have run an effective street-level campaign. The party sprang to life in the past month.

As Bolshoi has repeated at many of the group's well-attended rallies, "It's one thing to be held down by a feared dictator" – a reference to former president Mustafa Bleed – "but quite another to be held down by the absentee shadow of one."

If Bolshoi, now 71, seems an unlikely source of inspiration after decades in opposition, it's because many of his supporters are looking over his shoulders. People disappointed with Vadim Bleed have begun turning up for the inspired speeches of Lezer parliamentarian Fatma Gavras.

The doctor-turned-politician has captured the imagination of many disenfranchised citizens in the last 30 days. On the last day of campaigning, Gavras shared the stage with Bolshoi at every major event in the NNP schedule.

The pair began their morning at the Uranium Miners Association, whose workers have seen their hourly wages and on-the-job protections slashed as the foreign-owned mines reap record profits.

"She has our undying respect," said union leader Anatole Erdus. "Many of these workers first met Gavras when she treated their injuries after mining accidents. The Americans don't pay for the kind of care our injuries require. But Gavras has never asked for money from anyone."

At Revolution Square, Bolshoi and Gavras shared the stage and outlined their closing arguments before tomorrow's vote. "The revolution that started here is terminally ill," shouted Bolshoi, a reference to Blanco Bleed's signing of the Declaration of Sovereignty. "Call the doctor!" supporters chanted back in unison, as far back as the eye could see.

Mustafa Bleed

I LIKE TO TAKE MY BREAKFAST on the veranda, in the humid morning air, while reading *The Nation*. That way I know exactly how to abuse its editor during our daily exchange. A national newspaper, to my mind, should have priorities.

I'll tell you, quite honestly, I went through eight elections during my presidency. Eight. That's two more than my dad Blanco, who's practically a saint in this country and could have easily kept going had circumstances allowed it. I had landslides some years, others that required a bit of massaging, and each one of them provided its own unique challenge. But sitting on my hands like I have today, a VIP spectator with access to the front row, the green room, the cast, a firm hand on the director's shoulder, a pin on the producer's lapel, and yet no access to the stage itself, no full control of what's about to happen, leaving that all to Vadim, why, it's maddening.

This morning I woke up in a daze, after only four hours of sleep, which is as much as I can manage these days. The alarm was set to remind me that a lineup of pills stands behind it. I was already awake, staring at the ceiling. I sat up and ingested eight pills one by one, tongue, sip, swallow, repeat, until I could feel them burn down the lining of my leather stomach.

After breakfast, I had to go cast my vote before a strobe of camera flashes, if only for symbolic purposes. So, after I'd dressed, I ordered a helicopter to my rooftop's landing pad, and from there we soared above Qala Phratteh to the Ministry of the Interior. I like to sit up in front next to the pilot, Franco, whom I've known for many years, one of the Bleed family's longest-serving employees. Franco handed over the controls for a few minutes, because none of the pills I swallow every morning do as much to get my blood rushing like the sharp tilt of piloting an aircraft over Revolution Square, the warm wind rifling through my clothes like an overzealous border agent.

Have you ever seen the city in the morning from a helicopter? From up there, I can see the forested ridge of the Allegory Mountains encircling the capital, cradling an orange pillow of pollution. My father's statue marks Revolution Square, his sword rising up to cut the man-made cloud. There's only a hint of the eight boulevards leading out from the square. Today they were all lined with military trucks. The Bleed cinemas, the Bleed National Library, Bleed Stadium, the business district, the Lezer hovels, the copper waters of the Zafer River – you can tour it all with the turn of the steering stick, as if operating a surveillance camera.

Franco landed the helicopter on the roof of the Ministry of the Interior, and I leapt out as gingerly as one can at 82 with a bad leg and a cane, all the while holding down my silk tie against the rotor blades' gust. Inside, I took the elevators down to the main lobby where my bodyguard, a former wrestling protégé of mine, met me with the open arms of the son I never had. I donned sunglasses and limped into the public gallery to cast my vote before the state-sanctioned press corps. I flashed a quick victory sign as I pushed the voting card into the ballot box.

We disappeared into the private backrooms of the ministry. It was time for the morning's debriefing – a round table of the Bleed administration's executive committee, where I still hold a chair as Special Counsel to the President, a post I invented in the last months of my administration. I was impatient to get going, but I was trying my hardest to resist leading the meeting, out of deference to my son's image, and also out of respect to the staff who end up performing so much of the heavy lifting for which he invariably assumes credit. These days it's the General who carries most of the load, given that he's my longest-standing confidant and has been my right-hand man for almost three decades. That means that I confer with the General on many of the government's priorities, and he in turn controls much of what happens in this room, to my liking. So the meeting began when the General marched into the room, threw his officer's cap onto a coat rack and smacked the conference table with the palm of his hand.

"The day's not off to a good start," he said. "Lineups at polling stations are already longer than anticipated, and international observers are practically at every station. We should still have a fairly good idea of who's voting against us. The main objective of the day is to give the impression that Vadim is the natural man to beat. If we push back too hard today, he'll look weak."

Everyone around the table looked defeated already.

"If we can only get Vadim past this hurdle," I said, leaning forward, "then I'm sure over the next five years he's going to mature into his role. He'll turn 40 over the course of this coming term. I'm sure he'll settle in better than he already has."

For the next 30 minutes we discussed how to best get our voters out. With the help of my cane, I stood up and sighed. "Let's hope the day doesn't turn up too much trouble. Make sure our people get out and vote. If the opportunity arises to turn the situation in our favour, take it. At any sign of violence in unfriendly areas, shut down the polls. As far as we're concerned, our man is out front with the silent majority. At the end of the day, we'll take a look at the results and decide where to go from there. Those results do not leave this building without my say-so. Agreed?"

"Agreed," the ministers all said in unison, a spark of the discipline that used to occupy these halls on a daily basis.

After I adjourned the meeting, the General walked me down to my waiting limousine, and we reminisced about past elections along the way. The General and I have been through a lot together. On the drive back home, the limousine slipped through the silent streets of the normally bustling downtown core.

That evening, I tried my best not to show my worry at the state dinner. I worked the Bleed Ballroom with my usual flourishes, glad-handing ministers, stroking the egos of our American guests, all of them reticent senior managers of our uranium mines. These are the people who generously support our family and national programs with the land leases we've provided them, even though their government refuses to communicate with us officially. Tonight, their anxiety was hanging in the air like the smoke of so many cigars. No matter the subject of conversation, the refrain would return, often in little more than a whisper, "Your Excellency," because I'm cordial but not generous with our uranium-mining consortium, "my bosses back home would like assurances if President Vadim Bleed loses. We've invested so much here that…"

I know what you're thinking. At my age, five years removed from my 29-year run as President, shouldn't I be bronzing on the deck of a private yacht amongst the archipelagos of the Indian Ocean? I should've had more children, kept more options open for my succession. Shouldn't I be off enjoying my golden years, instead of pinch-hitting for Vadim? For that matter, shouldn't *he* be at this state dinner in the Bleed Ballroom?

Vadim Bleed

I VOTED FOR MYSELF THIS MORNING with only a 45-minute catnap in the back of the limo and some eye drops to prop me up. Once in the grand lobby and behind the velvet ropes that kept the cameras at bay, I checked off the little square next to my name, had some difficulty finding the slot in the ballot box, and then bowed to the good-natured applause of my entourage. Done! I must've looked like death, or at least a very attractive, sculpted version of it. My staff took over all unnecessary functions with all the precision of an emergency generator, and from then on I fell limp, only doling out the minimal movements required of my role.

I was finally free from public life again and more than happy to let my presence thrive in the collective psyche as a series of media quotables assembled by my team of surrogate voices. As I lay in the back of the limo and my personal assistant Isabella showered me with an unending torrent of data barf about regional vote forecasts, I inserted my discreet earbuds and relaxed to a playlist selection I'd put together well before the start of the campaign. The music felt old to me, devoid of any of the emotional flights I so badly needed. This campaign had robbed me of the time I usually invested in updating the music on my phone. I also hadn't driven my own car in much too long. The list of things I hadn't done was growing much longer than the list of the things I had.

My motorcade drove along the downtown streets, with the police up ahead and behind us blocking traffic and generally making sure that people were inconvenienced by my presence. I watched Isabella's lips moving fast through whatever she was explaining, and then turned up the volume on my Sade, whose voice I find soothing. I needed to calm down, catch a good night's rest finally. You must wonder where I go when I need to do that: how do I find my Zen spot at a moment's notice? The answer: I fall back on my racing days. I imagine myself hurtling up the hills of Monaco or through the warm rains of Tokyo at well over 200 km per hour, my right hand on the gearbox and my left on the wheel, feeling the car's movements as if they were extensions of my own body. Do you know I used to race over a hundred times a year? The Formula One circuit, the occasional NASCAR appearance, dune-buggy journeys across the Sahara, backwoods drag racing in Ukraine, Catalan stock-car demolition derbies, Israeli Motocross. I love the smell of morning dew at a track that hasn't yet been used that day. I adore the flare of diesel, the burn of tires on asphalt, shuddering along with the dials as the car pushes past its allotted potentials. There are no rules when you're driving that fast, there's no time for bureaucracy and committee meetings and for consensus and pleasing the people. There is only instinct, a razor-thin guide between glory and gore. Being president, I'm afraid, has pickled those instincts.

From the facing seat, Isabella tapped me with her pen. "You're not listening to me."

"No," I admitted, "I haven't been."

"Well, you're done for the day, so please get some rest."

When we got back to the presidential palace, I decided to take Isabella's advice: I needed a nap. The smell of clean sheets may as well have been an anaesthetic. I fell asleep instantly.

I woke up to the buzzing of my phone. It was still light out, and I had no idea how long I'd slept. I could've kept sleeping for days, but the phone kept buzzing. I ignored it and opted instead for a much-needed shower. My senses slowly thawed back into working order. There was that painful clarity I preferred to avoid, either the sharp fingernails of sobriety or a headache – I couldn't tell. That was when it occurred to me that the annoyances from my phone probably had something to do with the little mission I'd assigned my Minister of Sport and Leisure.

I checked the screen and sure enough he'd tried calling me fourteen times in the last four hours.

"Bruno, talk to me."

"I have a plane waiting on the runway."

"No more details now," I warned him, walking back to the bedroom window. "Tell me, how quickly can you get a helicopter over to the East Wing gardens?"

"From here, maybe twenty minutes."

"Do it."

I fumbled through my closet in search of a bag that would hold all I needed, and then fussed over the details of my suit in the closet's mirror. I looked good. Four hours of deep sleep had done wonders.

Sitting by the open bay window overlooking the gardens, I enjoyed the soft late-afternoon breeze as I listened to state radio and waited for my ride. State radio was reporting record turnout at the polls and only minimal violence. They predicted a comfortable Bleed victory. I didn't feel so bad taking off for a few days. And when I returned, I'd come bearing the gift of a brighter future for them, dangling it like the prize pheasant from a hunting trip.

Let me share a little secret with you. I can try all I want to shake loose my father's grip on this government, but no election will change that. To truly effect change, I need to tackle the people who line his pockets, and those of his police, his military, and his intelligence services. To jump-start our future, I've always thought, we need new uranium clients in the Allegory Mountains, new alliances that can push the old ones out of the way. And so I've been working on arranging such a meeting for months. I've secured interest to set the plan in motion.

A few days back, I met privately with an old acquaintance of mine from the London School of Economics, Jojo Babayev, the son of an Uzbeki cotton baron whom I remembered primarily for his Ping-Pong skills. We met at a rooftop club, while my schedule officially had me at a tennis match. I found him alone at the far end of a long table laid out for 24, in front of a large ashtray and an open carton of duty-free Marlboros. We reminisced about our university days for a while, and then he said, "Come, let's talk."

"Who's talking?" I asked.

"If all goes well, you'll soon find out."

"Whoever it is, they knew to send you instead of someone more official."

"The Americans are very sensitive right now. They're worried about the future of their land leases at the mines. My client doesn't want to ruffle feathers."

"Of course. The Americans have invested so much over the years."

"And now you want more."

"Sure. They've had the same terms on that land for three decades. No one in the world leases territory for that cheap anymore. We have new projects we want to invest in."

"But the Americans don't want to go there."

"We're negotiating. Nothing's set in stone."

"Right. Of course." He sat back and enjoyed a long haul of his Marlboro. "Tell me, Vadim, do you remember our Conflict Management lecture from third year? The professor, I forget his name, but he was a game theorist. He kept talking about the need to have control of the variables in any binding agreement. Do you remember that?"

"Vaguely."

"You must remember, I'm sure. He kept going on about how control is finite. In order to gain control, your opponent must first lose control," he began paraphrasing. "Control is a binding agreement that can only be disrupted by forces outside its participants. Those forces create a vacuum. The benefits of that vacuum fall to those who are best placed to take advantage in that moment. None of this strikes a chord?"

"Why is your client reading our old homework?"

"Because it's fascinating. Tell me, Vadim, do you know who controls your binding agreement?"

"Sure, we share a name."

"Maybe you need to let outside forces deliver a shock to what binds your controls. Allow its foundations to crumble a little, create your own vacuum."

"Is that what your client wants?"

"My client wants to help. You're at an uncertain juncture. The election, your father, the Americans…"

"You think there's a chance I might lose."

"I think it's important to do everything you can to ensure that those who would want you to lose don't get their way."

"And how can I do that when I'm about to have an election?"

"Have faith in the unexpected. Let someone who is outside the agreement help your cause. Leave the country. Don't be seen to be involved."

"The timing's bad."

"Opportunities shine brightest when no one is ready for them to appear. Finish your work and then book a distraction. Make it public enough so that we can find you without communicating. Once you're there, someone will be in touch."

"I'll see if my schedule allows for it."

"See that you do."

With that we stood. Jojo plastered a kiss on each of my cheeks, wedged his carton of duty-free Marlboros under his arm, and left.

I'd be lying if I said that conversation didn't remain with me. People don't normally approach the president with such schemes. We have attachés, ministers, underlings for that sort of thing. Sometimes it's best that I don't know the details and keep my nose out of the dirt. I'd spent five years working like that, being the smiling mannequin, the scarecrow really, in order to keep the whole operation humming along. Generally, I don't care; I'm good at being the one at the party who rockets down a champagne waterslide with the Duchess of Spain or takes MDMA with the deposed heir to the Ottoman throne in a centuries-old Turkish bath. A lot of good gets done in those instances that can set the whole bureaucratic machinery of both countries working towards a common goal. But this time it felt different. And maybe it's the fatigue of a month-long campaign thinking out loud here, but it felt thrilling to be in the driver's seat again. The prospect of wresting control from my father and changing course has dealt me a much-needed lifeline through this campaign flooded with insincere smiles, rote speeches, flashing cameras, and stingy handshakes. I could be a very different kind of president during this second term if only I could take more chances, get out from under Pa's thumb, the General's thumb, the many thumbs at our intelligence agencies, the glowing thumbs of our American uranium miners. I feel as though I've got thumbprints all over my face from the position I've been put into. The presidency I've inherited is like living inside the bronze-cast mould of my grandfather's statue. I've had to do a lot of contorting to fit into it. In my thoughts, Jojo's tantalizing offer had already set that scenario into motion. I couldn't go back, no matter what the election results.

How the fresh air felt good at that window overlooking the East Wing gardens. The lilies are in bloom, the pond is rippling, and in the distance I can hear only the faint bass of a poolside boombox. This country can captivate me so at times. Before I entered politics, ever since my school years really, I did most of my living outside – so many boarding schools, the London School of Economics, tournaments, rallies, vacations, appearances, endorsements, friends, parties, the entire network of Bleed seaside villas around the world. I didn't feel as compelled as I apparently do now to be here all that often. I was out there soaking up the world, as every eligible elite should do. But I've grown to appreciate it more, this little land of ours.

I sat there at the bay window and enjoyed that daydream for a short while, spacing out really. The breeze picked up at that magic hour and ruffled its fingers through my hair. The nap had left me dazed in a way that only made me want more. Soon the sound of chopping rotor blades filled the air. I watched the helicopter approach the palace grounds and carefully descend right before my window, tearing the heads off the garden lilies along the way. An attaché with a dossier in hand jumped out and ran around to where the palace security was approaching. After explaining himself over the deafening rotor blades, the security escorted him around the corner, most likely to find Isabella. Bruno had arranged it beautifully. I slipped down from the ledge and scampered across the grass to the helicopter, feeling as giddy as when I used to pull off this kind of escape artistry back in boarding school. Of course, the helicopter I had back then was much smaller than the one I have now.

National Election Complete,
Warring Bleed Factions Resume Clashes

by Kaarina Faasol

Well, it didn't take very long at all for the Bleeds to start slashing at each other's throats again. They've been behaving themselves for a full month now, putting up a united front for those pesky international observers that have been snooping around, and of course for that Boran public of theirs, which shouldn't be given the opportunity to splinter in the face of a rising opposition that earnestly wants their vote.

But one day after the election (just one day!) sources at *The Nation*, who are barred from reporting such news, tell me that father and son have unleashed their toy armies, and that these jeep-bound bands of former military men-for-hire are roaming neighbourhoods in broad daylight, exchanging machine-gun fire much to the dismay of a very frightened public. One child, nine years old, was sent to hospital with a bullet to the thigh, and an elderly woman had to be treated for shock.

Readers of this space will note that this is a return to normal and not a new development. Father and son have been locked in a behind-the-scenes power struggle for several years now. Sources inside the vast government bureaucracy know very well that the elder Bleed only ever wanted his son to be president in name, and that the easily bored younger Bleed has bristled at the idea of being the pretty face to his father's conniving brain ever since he was a child.

They are cordial if and when they have to share a room. Mustafa Bleed agreed to throw his weight behind his son's first presidential run with the caveat that the elder Bleed would maintain control of the more valuable cabinet posts. Initially Vadim didn't appear to care. He enjoyed the attention and curiosity of the campaign the way any career racer would. But no driver wants to feel like a puppet in public, especially when it's his father's hand reaching up his behind and into his mouth.

Both have been known to employ militias to send each other nasty messages. It all began, we're told, after father very publicly scolded son during one of the latter's rare appearances at a cabinet meeting. Insulted, Vadim had his men go round to his father's kennels and slit the throats of the old Dobermans he so infamously brought to parliamentary sessions. Mustafa retaliated by having his men blow up one of his son's race cars. And it has continued like that for a few years now, their men growing to despise each other. Now no one's sure who's calling the shots anymore, if orders come from Bleeds or if squadron leaders further down the chain are going rogue.

President Bleed's spokesperson has downplayed the latest scuffle. "As you're well aware," came the written response to queries from editors of *The Nation*, "now that the election is over, the president has quickly resumed business as usual while the nation awaits the results of the vote. He's currently in Europe for meetings on future trade agreements that require his personal attention. He has no need or desire to see these sorts of street-level charades continue when the rest of the world is beckoning us into the 21st century."

Touché. For their part, officials in the New Nationalists Party see an all-too-familiar cycle of provocation and distraction rising up again. "The country should be demanding a fair and transparent vote count," says Lezer spokesperson Fatma Gavras. "Instead, their roving gangs are out in the streets intimidating people with their dangerous theatrics. And the ballots are hidden away, being manipulated as we speak."

International UN observers have reported incidents of ballot stuffing in the regions south of the capital. The Bleed government has issued no statement since the election, claiming only that the turnout was higher than expected and the count could take days as results continue to stream in from more remote corners of the territory.

In the meantime, work at the region's extensive uranium mines in the Allegory Mountains has ground to a halt as we all wait to see which way the political winds will blow next. Minister of the Interior Constantin Benini is once again grumbling about American intervention – a traditional pressure tactic that has been used time and again to distract the public at times of social unrest.

Mustafa Bleed

NEVER IN MY 82 YEARS have I wanted to pin an election down to the mat like the one we're grappling with today, and leave it behind. Have you seen the coverage in *The Nation*? Listen to this! "*NNP opposition candidate Dabny Bolshoi has tried to tap into the frustrations of voters who have not loved Bleed as much as they did his grandfather Blanco, nor respected him as they did his father Mustafa.*" Of course it's true that I was deeply respected, that my father was loved, but these tabloid journalists, hacks every last one of them, have hijacked the very newspaper my father founded and are using its pages to spit in our faces! Why don't we just start paying all Dabny's election expenses while we're at it? It's infuriating what Vadim lets them get away with writing these days.

I read that article before bed last night, as I was watching yet another demonstration materialize beneath my residence on Revolution Square. These are the long-term consequences of Vadim's inattentiveness. He can talk all he wants about loosening the reins and allowing our institutions to modernize, and we can all have a laugh at the flirting and fun he pantomimes in public, but the whole time disease is spreading under the skin of the nation.

I slept badly, trawling through a swamp of revenge fantasies, and I woke up too early this morning. I was out of bed before my alarm. Sometimes I think my medications are too strong. When I'm awake in the middle of the night, feeling defeated by my offspring, I wonder if I'm not too old for this. Shaky hands, liver spots, turkey neck, a hunch, a paunch – I should have invested in finding a cure for ageing when I was younger. Plastic surgery can only pull back my skin so far. But modern medicine has yet to find a sustainable method for beautifying my enlarged prostate, grafting the muscle tissue of a young bull onto these aging arms, or injecting these brittle bones with molten iron. I should just let this entire region spiral off without me, put on the blinders. Of course I can't. This is Bleed country, my father's invention, my life's work, Vadim's responsibility, our family's legacy.

Unable to idle in my penthouse any longer, I decided to forego the blustery morning breeze of the rooftop helipad, and instead requested that my chauffeur ready the limo. I had to get to the Ministry of the Interior and find out how the vote count was going.

As we drove along Qala Phratteh's main boulevards, I felt depressed. The election's aftermath littered the streets.

"Why must they burn cars?" I complained.

I hadn't seen the downtown this empty in many years. No one dared step out. Along the boulevard lay shells of burnt-out oil drums, shards of shattered shop windows, splinters of cracked two-by-fours, and the rusty markings of dried blood. At one point, we had to slow down the limo to manoeuvre around an overturned military jeep. As we approached the government district, I noticed that the General had taken the extraordinary measure of putting up a checkpoint. We paused at the barbed-wire barricade straddling both lanes of the boulevard, while my driver flashed our security clearance at the soldier on duty, who advised us that, all in all, it wasn't a good day to go out driving.

Farther inside the security perimeter, the buildings appeared to crawl back to life, with the odd sight of an open window, a parked car with a driver waiting outside, smokers standing on the stairs of our electricity consortium. We pulled up to the Ministry of the Interior, which had more guards out front today.

Once inside, my old Minister of Finance fell in line with me as I strode down the corridor.

"The General is in a bad mood," he warned. "He's been up half the night putting out fires all across the country, people burning down polling stations, a post office ransacked in the north."

"Where is he now?"

"Still in the ballot vaults. Should I send a page to let him know you're here?"

"No need. I'm going down there now."

Have you ever seen where ballots go to get counted? Four floors underground, beneath the underground garage, two different security clearances, armed guards standing at attention, a thumb scan, and a finally a secret handshake with an elderly doorman who's been there since the Blanco days. It's his invention of course, but if you can't nail the intricate fingerplay, he's been known to not let you through. I throw in a bear hug at the end, because we go way back and there aren't many people left in these halls who personally knew my father.

The ballot vault is the size of a gymnasium. Its lacquered wooden floors were lined with long tables where Ministry of the Interior employees were busy organizing just-returned ballot boxes in the sections representing their regions. The large pink ballot sheets were everywhere you turned, on the floors, in the garbage bins, stacked high, crumpled up in balls. On the small stage in the back, I found the General slumped in a folding chair, his blazer hanging off the back and his sleeves rolled up.

"How bad?" I said, my hand on his shoulder. "Don't sugar-coat it."

"We haven't counted everything yet. We've only made in-roads on Qala Phratteh, not the regions."

"Qala Phratteh is where we normally do well."

"We're not."

"In any case, we keep counting. If we need extra ballots to even things out, we have them. If we need to lose some ballots, then we can do that too. We have as many empty ballots as garbage cans, so it should all balance out in the end."

"The other ministries are beginning to smell a problem. We've been fielding calls all morning about what to do in the event of a transition, what files to destroy, what happens in case of an emergency."

"Keep counting for now. It's a long process. No one expects you to announce results today."

"*The Nation* does. They've been clamouring for results. Not to meddle in family matters, but if you could have a talk with your son, get him more involved in all this, we'd all be grateful."

"Do you really want him running around down here?"

We both sighed.

"Keep up the good work." I patted him on the back. The General and I have been through a lot together.

I spent the rest of the morning in Vadim's office, fielding calls from frustrated mining officials unsure how to read the most recent tensions. It turns out many of them have been dealing with sabotage in the last few days, workers talked into not showing up, vandalizing the heavy machinery, New Nationalists graffiti. This morning, apparently, the car of one of our foreign senior managers was set on fire.

"It's theatre," I reasoned. "They do this because they know you'll get scared and call me. Don't buy into their cheap pressure tactics. We will compensate you generously for the damages when this all passes."

I hung up the phone, exhausted by all the lying that had to be done to keep everything on track. Sitting back in my old chair, looking out on the marble courtyard outside the window, my old view, I couldn't help but wonder if the country wouldn't be better off if I were still in charge.

It's history now, but I first stepped into the presidency unexpectedly, under extraordinary circumstances, and almost right away I had a virulent Lezer uprising to confront. I had to improvise, learn on the go. The administration left behind by my father was a mess. I had to rebuild it all. I didn't want to put Vadim through that. He's not made the same way. I knew that if he was to follow in my footsteps at all, then he had to be eased into the job. He was wild as a boy, all over the place. He didn't have the easiest of childhoods. You can't control much of what your children will have to endure. I don't want to get into details or sound like I'm making excuses for a grown man. But how I'd hate it if that one act of generosity should, in the end, unravel all I've built.

I decided to leave the Ministry and head back home, call in my personal trainer and hole up in my penthouse's private gym.

There's so much anxiety raging through my sore back muscles. There I'll alternate between bench presses, sparring exercises, a Turkish massage, and some soul-searching in the sauna.

The General ordered two unmarked cars to escort us back. "We'd rather play it safe," he stressed.

Two black sedans pulled up with four agents in each. We all drove to the government's barbed-wire perimeter. Outside the barricade, the streets were once again eerily silent, even though by then it was the middle of the afternoon. As we drove along, the stillness around us was so conspicuous that I could feel that we were being watched from behind the boarded-up shop windows and closed-off curtains.

"I haven't seen it like this since the '87 elections," I said to the driver. "How old were you in '87?"

"Two, sir."

"Then you don't remember." It occurred to me, as we drove along, that this tension in Qala Phratteh was instigated by those who were too young to know the full weight of a Bleed government's powers, and that they were being manipulated by the few old faces left in the rebel wings, who sensed that Vadim was the weak link they'd been waiting for all these years.

"Don't these people have to work?" I complained.

"People are waiting for results," said the driver, navigating through a pack of stray dogs lazing about in the empty streets. "No one knows what to do next."

"These dogs are going to take over. Where is animal control? They should at least be working."

"The General has called them off for now," said the driver. "He doesn't want easy targets on the street."

The dogs began to run alongside our motorcade, tongues lapping as they barked at us. They reminded me of the Dobermans I once owned, such fearsome animals, yet so loyal when properly trained, unlike my son. Then one dog exploded, and the car almost veered off the road. Immediately I ducked down. From the floor of the speeding car, I could see that the window opposite me had been blown out. I was covered in dog meat.

Vadim Bleed

ONE OF MY FAVOURITE PLACES to sit back and reflect is in my private jet, looking out the window at the permanent sunshine that lives above the clouds. I aspire to that state of mind every day. People in the VIP rooms of the world's nightclubs will often ask, "Doesn't the never-ending nag of the presidency worry you?" I always reply, "Stress is a choice. You can either be beneath the clouds getting rained on, in the clouds groping for direction, or above the clouds, in control, the big picture at your feet."

"Scotch, Mr. President?" asked the in-flight cocktail waitress.

"Single-malt on ice, something peaty, a touch of water. Thank you."

She disappeared behind the curtain.

With my head once again focused, I'm now quietly excited for the day ahead. According to my press agent, the distraction that was arranged is a photo shoot for the Austrian edition of *Cosmopolitan*. So in a couple of hours we'll be landing in Vienna to ride stallions bareback or hang perilously from studio-built cliffs.

I wouldn't accept such invitations if I weren't in good company. The Grand Duke of Luxembourg, the Sovereign Prince of Monaco (a great friend and billiards enthusiast), the ambiguous – and ambidextrous – Crown Prince of Thailand. It should make for a unique networking opportunity. The proximity at these things, ploughing past so many levels of bureaucracy, can lead to great advances for a small country like ours. I've signed many a trade deal on the inside of a forearm.

"Here you are," said the cocktail waitress, setting the whisky down.

She blushed. Once I was sure she was out of earshot, I reached for my briefcase and pulled out my satchel of mobile phones. I have four in total. All the better to compartmentalize with.

There's a blogger out there, a Kaarina Faasol who's been writing these posts on a site called Transfusion Blog – I can't help but roll my eyes every time I think of the dim light bulb that must have lit up when that little bit of wordplay struck. She's been writing garbage about me day in and day out. I need to touch base with Zaan, my man on the ground. Zaan is good Boran people. He's a squadron commander in the Intelligence Services. We go way back.

I dialled a number and was immediately directed to an answering machine. "Fox to Falcon," I said, and then hung up. A moment later, the phone vibrated.

"What's going on down there?"

"They were baiting us, boss."

"You know it's all over the Internet. They say that me and Pa can't go one day without fighting. Like a soap opera, for god's sake."

"It's not like other times," Zaan said. "We keep hearing things. There may be an operation underway. Maybe from inside."

"An operation," I lowered my voice, just in case. "What kind of operation?"

"Against you. Against us."

"They smell weakness. It's all these shit-disturbing rumours that people are reading. Someone's spreading damaging information."

"Your news agency is volatile. This Nada Ferber writes stories *The Nation* can't publish and passes them on to people outside. She's the only one with that kind of access. But we don't fight street battles for journalists. It's your father. There's a recording."

"And?"

"He's discussing making moves."

"He wouldn't."

"He thinks he has the support. Said we should be careful."

"Take care of it. I'll stay away in the meantime. And take care of this news problem, please. This blog is such an eyesore when I travel."

"Of course, boss."

I hung up, and I tried not to get upset. With an important photo shoot coming up, I can't afford to have my face puff up and my temper poison my otherwise cool and collected presence. That kind of thing gets magnified by the camera. Dads have a way of getting under your skin and staying there, don't they? Where does this chip come from, I wondered for the ten millionth time while staring blankly at the bright blue circle of sky outside.

It's not like we spent much time together when I was growing up – I was in boarding schools most of the time, or under the guidance of my uncles, an ever-changing carousel of despondent male nannies. My father was always putting down uprisings or touring the world's ambassadorial palaces, work I understand now but resented back then.

Forgive my getting personal, but there's so much entangled love and hate coursing through my veins. As a little boy, I feared him. Do you know he used to come into my room late at night, when I was sleeping, and get me out of bed, shove me into his one-seat race car so that I was trapped between the steering wheel and his cognac-drenched breath as he sped through the streets? Tears would stream back toward my ears in the open car as the air rushed past and woke me up to the full horror of where I was. All the while, he'd be whispering these awful platitudes in my ear about power and manhood. And what do I do? I go on to race cars around the world, rocketing mounds of steel across asphalt as if tempting death. The cars I've crashed trying to kill that one memory.

Bruno poked his head in from behind the curtain divide and asked if everything was okay. Apparently, I'd started cursing aloud during that overlong bad memory. Truth be told, I was in a sour mood. I try not to get stressed out, but on days like these, when some people feel intent on bringing me down, it's hard to resist.

"It's my father," I confessed, polishing off my whisky.

"Are you stressed?" he asked, as if he could smell it in the cabin.

"Nothing good can come of stress," I lamented. "Not one single good decision has ever been made in a moment of stress."

"Why don't we do some yoga? In fact, I advise you, as your minister, to join me in stretching out your core and learning to breathe. I'll lead."

I had him call in the stewardess to join us, to make us a group. I always find yoga more calming that way.

"Ommmm," Bruno chanted, pushing his pelvis off the floor.

"Ommmm," we followed suit.

THE NATION

MAHBAD'S NEWS SOURCE SINCE 1964

Election Results Delayed

Government suggests international conspiracy

BY NADA FERBER

Two days after record turnout at the polls, results are still not available.

The Ministry of the Interior has issued a statement citing logistical obstacles in ballot deliveries from the regions as the main problem. But unofficially, sources from the Ministry suggest irregularities in voting that could point to international interference.

At issue is a delegation of 121 foreign observers, whose presence during the election the opposition New Nationalists Party coordinated with the United Nations. Ever since, the government has argued that an international conspiracy was forming against the Bleed family.

The basis of these allegations stems from President Vadim Bleed's protracted negotiations with SUMCAX, the international uranium-mining conglomerate. The lack of progress in those talks has led to government threats of nationalization.

Minister of the Interior Constantin Benini said American mining officials have convinced their government to pressure the UN into allowing observers in order to weaken Bleed's position in the negotiations.

"We want to ensure fair elections as much as anyone," said Benini in a brief press conference. "But every move comes with consequences. You can't fight for international observers and not expect a whole raft of issues from the country's international portfolio to be affected. Everything is related. So now we have to be very careful with the votes that were collected and investigate every suspicion to be certain that foreign entities have not corrupted our democratic integrity."

Given ongoing investigations into allegations of interference and the delay of ballots arriving from the regions, the Bleed government estimates that citizens may have to wait upwards of a week for results to be announced. President Bleed's office has issued a statement calling for calm as the results are vetted and tallied.

A wait that long is highly unusual, says presidential candidate and opposition leader Dabny Bolshoi. He believes the government is stalling for time because Vadim Bleed lost the vote by a wide margin. "The Bleed government is floundering for a method to doctor the results. All their tried and tested methods failed to take into account how deeply unpopular the Bleeds have become. No matter how they tally it up, the votes in their favour keep coming up short."

NNP parliamentarian Fatma Gavras has called for demonstrations tonight at Revolution Square. "We called on international observers to ensure fairness, but then the Bleeds walked away with all the votes and have decided to do whatever they like. I guarantee you this election is being stolen."

Benini advises citizens against attending any post-election protests. In recent days, the city has seen a rash of small-scale bombings. "We fear that any mass gathering will open the door to extreme elements looking to take advantage."

The Ministry of the Interior says persons of interest have been arrested. NNP has reported that two of its candidates are among the arrests. The government reports that both candidates have a history of involvement with Lezer rebel groups.

The Ministry maintains that Vadim Bleed's unpopularity is exaggerated, and is based on an over-amplification of a vocal minority.

Mustafa Bleed

AS A FATHER, I FEEL RESPONSIBLE for my son; how could I not? A small part of me intuitively takes responsibility for his actions or, regrettably, his lack of actions. Now Vadim's missing in action again as *The Nation* runs rampant with cheap poison about election fraud and opposition views. The NNP's purpose, need I remind you, as it's written in the constitution, is to support and improve the image of the ruling party, not desecrate it. To offer a release valve to those poor souls impoverished by righteousness. That's what an opposition should do! Not these fatalistic demonstrations in the square I built for the memory of my dear father. How am I expected to look out my windows at night when there's a sea of bed-sheet banners gathered around the bronze statue of my father on horseback, and jeering megaphones chanting *Call the doctor* and *We want blood on our hands*? This all happened before, 30 years ago, at around the same point in my presidency, and it took me four full years to tamp the lid back down. And I was here the whole time, actively engaging the dissidents, banning discontent, arresting people, making persons of interest disappear, delivering dire warnings in public speeches, making sure the country knew beyond any reasonable doubt who was in charge.

Forgive me, I'm rambling, I know. It's been a rough day, my stomach is acting up, and the medications I've taken are raging through me with side effects. I've had this burning pain on my right side, just below my rib cage, ever since this afternoon. Where to start? The results are bad, worse off than anyone thought possible. I spent the morning at the Ministry of the Interior going over the numbers with the General, and we were both dismayed by how out of control the situation has become in five years. We huddled in my old office, the pages of the confidential vote report splayed on the desk between us, trying to figure out how to do something about the numbers.

"A 68/32 breakdown against us is unheard of," I complained. "I've never seen anything like it. We had, what, a 53/47 split last time. How could Vadim lose 15% of the population?"

"Last time, Mustafa, people took your word about him. He looked good in a race car. They thought, well, it's more of the same. Why not? And a 6% difference isn't hard to work with when you have a voter turnout of just over 50%."

I shuffled through the pages. "And the participation rate this time?"

"82%"

"That's a bit unrealistic, don't you think? Were we letting the exploding dogs vote?"

"Sadly, this is what happens when every single Lezer in the country feels motivated to vote. Add to that New Nationalists collecting all the other outlawed opposition groups under one banner, so they vote for a change. They say people are unhappy. In most people's view, Vadim doesn't show up. He's not even doing a bad job – he's not doing a job at all."

"You know, Constantin, I like to think that I grew into my father the older I got. That I took on his qualities, and began

44

to think like him. I've been waiting for Vadim to do the same, but it's beginning to look like too much of that was selfish hope. Where did I go wrong with him?"

"We can work with a less-than-perfect leader for one generation. We just need a likeable-enough figurehead for the theatrical parts. Someone who shows up for the job is enough."

"Can we massage these numbers?" I asked blankly.

"With 82% showing up, there's not enough room to stuff the ballot boxes in our favour."

"What are our options, then?"

"Well, Vadim could concede."

"You mean lose. You want a Bleed to lose the nation we founded. If I were still president, I'd call that treason and you'd be gone, just like that."

"But Vadim is president and he's never here."

"We need one more term. He's only 37. If I push harder, I can change him, make him better."

"I have every confidence you could."

"God damn it, why did I retire? We'd never be in this situation if I were still president."

"No, we wouldn't."

"Worst move of my career. At the time I was thinking only of the family, but now I feel like I threw it all away."

"Well, maybe next time you could run against Vadim," he laughed, though I sense he was only half-joking. I laughed too, but inside we were both considering it.

"Until we get there," I finally replied, "we'll have to make do with the cards we've got."

"I think we've got a case to make with the international interference angle. If we could get to a second vote then…"

"A runoff?"

"For example."

"I could propose that to parliament. I think we could muster enough momentum if it comes from me. People owe me favours."

"It'll look messy, but at least we'll get to where we need to go."

We decided that a second vote, called quickly, without international observers, would be the best way forward. With a strategy in hand, I spent the rest of the morning in the sauna. I have the mind of a Ferrari. But these days, what with the pills, the limp, and the years of grappling, it's been stuffed under the dented hood of a rusting Yugo.

I was profoundly irritated, and as is usually the case when I'm irritated, I call Vadim. Lo and behold, once again I got his voicemail. What is the point of a mobile phone if you never answer it, I ask you. I left a long and forceful message that spelt out for him, in no uncertain terms, how I would take the presidency away from him like his favourite toy if he didn't shape up, listen to his pa, come home, and act like the Bleed he was supposed to be. Someone has to take control.

Vadim Bleed

AFTER LISTENING TO PA'S LATEST tirade, I've grown despondent. I didn't know what to make of Zaan's revelations about recordings where the old man daydreams about replacing me. But that phone message pretty much confirmed it all for me. We're dead set against each other, we always have been. Our shared blood should have tempered our anger, but instead it's amplified everything. So now I'm walking around in the dark of my Viennese hotel room, sulking like the little boy I never wanted to be, and every step I take is greeted by motion-detecting floor lamps that light up as I approach. They provide just enough light so that I don't have to think about groping for a light switch in the dark. But when I look behind me, they dim and disappear. The concept is beautiful in its simplicity, really. Only as much light as you'll ever need. More light than my pa ever provided in my childhood, in any case.

I could use some cheering up. To that end, I've just had the hotel wake up their star chef and sommelier to devise a special taster's menu, something fresh, different, spontaneous. I feel lonely. Funny how that feeling works: when it's on your mind, it's all you want to tell someone, anyone. You know, whenever

I travel the world and meet people, ladies in particular, whenever I deliver a casual foot massage or trot across a disco's dance floor or fluff a one-night-stand's hotel pillows, I get asked, "Why aren't you with someone? Why hasn't that special someone come along?" Or my advisors will say, "Vadim, a president ought to have a first lady to soften the sharp edges."

My Bulgarian mother, Bryn, the first woman in my life, she spoiled me for the rest. They say, in the mythical story of my early life, that she was unhappy, arranged into marriage by her father and my grandfather, a convenience of the times for one and an opportunity for the other. My pa needed someone to tenderize his image, just as he says I should follow suit now, for the sake of the bloodline. But then I think of all that I would have traded away for a mother happier than the one I got.

They say I was an overwhelming breastfeeder who suckled long after infancy. Or that's how the woman who never wanted to feed me described it once on state television. The whole country knew this fact because Bryn went on my pa's TV show and complained about having to raise me. I see now she felt trapped in the marriage and I was a shackle for her. I see how she would say anything to wound him, just like I would. She'd humiliated me before I knew the meaning of the word. Pa pushed back too hard. It was national television after all, and here was this Bulgarian princess who was much too tall to be taken seriously by the proudly short Boran political elite, pretty much unloved by her public, bemoaning the heir apparent. He snapped, made some very nasty remarks about arranged marriages and Bulgarians. She left for exile shortly after that. One of my earliest memories is of suckling desperately at those last meagre drops. Her body must have already been preparing to

48

abandon me, as I was only getting runoff by then. Then she pulled me from her chest like a leech, a plump bubbly know-nothing, only eleven sharp teeth in all, curiously bleary from buttery breast milk in my eyes, wondering why my mum was giving me a contemptuous, disapproving glare as she buttoned up her nursing bra for the last time, her blouse, her waistcoat, and without even a goodbye kiss on the forehead, walked down the runway to her waiting plane.

They say she didn't even leave extra bottles for the weaning. I was left to grapple at the chest of any woman in my perimeter, many of whom were intimidated secretaries or scandalized foreign diplomats, as I was only ever allowed to visit my pa's presidential offices for an hour every day. My thirst was beginning to infringe on national interests. To break my all-consuming addiction, Pa prescribed only male nannies.

I know what you're thinking. They always blame their mothers. Behind the stately official portraits, their inner lives are so messy. History has landed squarely on my side, with new reports of all the rich nutrients I'd sapped her of early on. She was wrong to deny me more, and it's difficult for me to speak about it.

Painstakingly I outgrew my predilection. At boarding schools around the world, I was able to explore my blossoming sexuality as freely as I liked, either by paying off my ever-looming bodyguards or enlisting them in the endeavours. From the age of eleven on, after lights-out at the dormitories, I would sneak out with the help of some ex-wrestler who'd moved into the shady world of personal security. We'd drive my appointed limo to the nearby tavern or the city's red-light district in search of willing women who, sufficiently curious by the prospect of seeing the interior of the car, would let me fondle and caress them as they stroked my hair. I wept softly in their humid embraces, and they said things like "There, there, little man, you're going to be all right."

It's amazing what a young imagination can unleash at the very beginnings of a boy's sexual wanderlust, especially when there are no parents to bother with and no budgets to worry about. The saunas of Sweden or the sweat lodges of Nunavut, the Ferris wheels of Buenos Aires or the Byzantine chapels of Chechnya, I've turned away from no adventure in my desire to tease, tantalize, trespass. In exchange, I've gained only emptiness. That bond they speak of, the one that can tether two people together, is either a lie or beyond my grasp. I tried to buy it, and ended up purchasing only veiled actresses who inevitably tired of my unique habits and refunded my money. I was sixteen by then, lost in a funhouse of poorly conceived experiments and unexpected accidents. I had left behind me only an increasingly troublesome trail of litigation for my pa's lawyers to sort through. Pa's Minister of Justice blamed my half-Bulgarian blood for the perverted outlook. When Pa bought me my first private plane for my seventeenth birthday, all I could think was to fly to that convent in Bulgaria where my mum was cloistered, meet her, confront her, learn from her, find a way to shut down the sparkling sapphire mine of sadness that had dug this massive hole in my life, and be done with it.

Bryn was not at all who I remembered her to be. The 15 years since I'd last seen her, stowing away her frigid breast on that windy runway, had transformed her into someone I barely recognized. I suppose I remembered the tall, glamorous, well-dressed first lady I had framed in the two pictures on my dormroom dressers. When I finally arrived at the convent, I waited hours before I was finally allowed to meet with her.

She's been resting, I was told. She needs to sleep whenever the opportunity arises.

"Mum," I said, "I hope you got enough rest." She looked like someone battered by the world.

"Not really," she said. "I wasn't able to get back to sleep once they told me you were here."

"Why didn't you just get up and come see me?"

"I was hoping you'd go away."

"You don't want me here," I said, embarrassed.

"You can stay if you insist. But not for long. There's no room for you here."

"That's not fair. You have no idea who I am."

"I know that you're your father's son, that's enough. I know that your father murdered many people, a whole generation of Lezer boys, men, your age, younger, gone. I know that I can't have that on my conscience. I know that if you stay here long enough, you'll attract attention and your father's problems will come back to haunt me. I know what you must still be denying to yourself, that you can never be just you, that you will always be a prize for those who need you, an anchor for those who don't."

At the time, I didn't know what she was talking about. I didn't know what a Lezer was, or why my pa had killed so many of them. "But I am me," I insisted. "I'm no one else but me! I didn't kill anyone."

She only shook her head sadly as if I would never understand. "Whether you recognize it or not, his demon is in you."

"I want him out, Mum! Help me, please." I was kneeling at her bedside by then, tears streaming down my face.

"I don't know that you can be helped," she said, sitting up and touching my forehead to see if she could sense a will to change.

51

"I love you. You see a part of me I've never known before. I'll do anything to make it right again. Anything."

"Don't be unrealistic. You can't bring back all those people."

"But I can be my own person," I cried. "I believe I can."

"Then you must cut the cancer from your soul before it matures. You must give yourself to God."

I was baptized for the first time. My mum tied me to a bed. Over the next four days she prayed for me. She covered me with handfuls of ashes from an old urn. She gave me water from a sponge. And when it was finally over, she untied my bruised wrists and ankles, and embraced my half-conscious body for the first time, as if I was a new person, and I felt better for her acceptance of me, but I could still feel a static sameness inside.

A discreet knock at the door. The first course has arrived, carted up to be introduced by the chef himself. I see before me a miniature statue of scallops on a wire frame, seared on one side. The scallop figurine is set into a quicksand of lemon- and orange-peel compote. He appears to be looking over his shoulder.

"Can he not see the trap of the wakame seaweed forest around him?" the chef asked rhetorically.

"It's a beautiful opening salvo," I said sullenly, recognizing my own fate in his creation.

"Of course, sir."

The chef left to prepare the second course. I was alone again, staring at the scallops, which looked as downtrodden as I did the day I left that convent. Desperately I resolved to meet one of these Lezers whose fates had affected my mum so deeply. Who were they, I wondered, and why were they so significant in my parents' separation. I grew obsessed, could think of nothing else. I bribed the superintendent at my all-boys academy in Rome and was promptly introduced to a Lezer girl named Valencia who was attending our sister school.

We began fooling around. Perhaps it was because my mum had freed something inside me during those four days, but Valencia was the first girl my age I'd paid any attention at all, and I fell in love with her. For the very first time, I felt close to another person, I could see a future with her, and that vision made me feel more complete. But when her parents found out who I was, they forbade her from having anything to do with me.

"Tell them they have no idea who I am," I said when she told me.

"It doesn't matter who you are," Valencia said. "My father says we didn't go through hell and back just so I could put them all in danger once again."

They moved her to a boarding school in Copenhagen. I followed Valencia in my private plane, boiling over with youthful passion for this person I simply had to possess, and it must've been then that she got pregnant. Her mother cried for a long time when she found out. Her father threatened to move her halfway around the world. I assured them that their daughter would become one of the richest women in our country, and that she would be cared for eternally, as would they.

"I'm going to marry Valencia. The troubles of your generation are not ours."

"You're a spoiled child," her father said. "You know nothing, and your ignorance will destroy us all."

I burned with a desire to prove them wrong. I even told my pa. "I'm in love with her, she's a Lezer, and we're going to have a baby. Our baby will change our homeland, make it a better place."

And unlike Valencia's father, the old man appeared resigned to the fact that I was going to do what I wanted to do. Still, nine days later Valencia was struck by a speeding car on her way to the grocery store. She later died in hospital. The driver was never located.

A few months after that, I received word that Bryn had been committed to a psychiatric institution for conducting too many exorcisms. Her mind had been faltering for many years, and she had begun to see demons in everyone she encountered. In exchange for signing some forms stating that I would not pursue legal action against the church, I was offered a generous compensation package.

Tensions Spike Across Qala Phratteh

Government withholds results as demonstrations grow

BY NADA FERBER

Opponents of President Vadim Bleed clashed again with police last night after a rally at Revolution Square. Thirteen people have died as a result of election-related violence in the past 24 hours.

More than 130 people have been arrested since Tuesday's election, according to police figures, and nearly another hundred have been injured.

Eyewitness reports described a frenzied and vocal crowd that swelled beyond the square. The battle between protestors and police lasted well into the morning.

Three opposition candidates have gone missing. Plainclothes officers took them from their homes in the night, according to their families. The government claims to have no information about their whereabouts and

cited complex tribal dynamics between Lezers and Borans in the regions as a possible reason.

The thousands gathered at Revolution Square were a show of force that will be difficult for the Bleed government to ignore as the whereabouts of election ballots continue to hang in the air. New Nationalists Party candidates arrived at the historic plaza in the late afternoon, covering their mouths with black bandanas to illustrate the loss of their democratic voice.

"We are in the dark," said Bleed rival Fatma Gavras, who gave a speech and led the candidates in chants. "We voted, and the ballots have essentially disappeared from view." The demonstration quickly attracted students from the nearby university. "We voted for New Nationalists because, with Vadim, we'll have no jobs," said one student who requested anonymity for fear of retaliation.

, Fouad, an 86-year-old retired mathematics professor who refused to give his surname, was drawn to the demonstration out of concern for the missing ballots. "With Blanco, there was hope and we had the feeling we could grow. But with Mustafa, things got worse. We had extremists, terrorism. The situation with uranium got worse. His people, the Borans, got wealthy. Everyone else, especially the Lezers, suffered."

At 10 p.m., the police cordoned off Revolution Square and advanced on the demonstrators. NNP supporters and the student protesters say they'll be back tomorrow and every night after that, until the election results are revealed. Several labour unions have planned to join them.

Meanwhile, sources within the Ministry of the Interior say the Bleed administration is building a case for international interference. According to staffers within the Ministry, who spoke on condition of anonymity, General Constantin Benini and former president Mustafa Bleed are circulating drafts of a plan for a run-off vote among Bleed Party parliamentarians.

The government charges there is evidence linking observers to the uranium-mining conglomerate that's currently deadlocked in negotiations with the Bleed administration.

General Benini refused to address the government's plans, other than to say that former president Mustafa Bleed, now a special advisor to his son, will address parliament tomorrow with more details.

Mustafa Bleed

OH, THIS BUSINESS WITH *The Nation* is getting so tedious! When my poor, saintly, late father envisioned a national newspaper, he imagined a daily update of the government's affairs, freely available to all. I'm sorry, I'm not the type to complain, but have you seen the latest edition? I'm bringing it to parliament to make an example of that gutter-press editor who we've allowed to run such a venerable and necessary institution. This lax attitude toward trash is, to me, the reason behind all that's wrong in this country. Heads will roll.

"Nada Ferber wants to start a war," I shouted into the receiver as we drove along the empty streets of the government district. "It's treason. Execute her."

"She has a Norwegian passport," the General lamented. "We'd have a diplomatic headache on our hands."

"Arrest her, deport her, cut off her fingers. There must be something we can do. My father's own gift to our people is being used against us. We should already be at war. We could wrap up this whole mess in a matter of hours."

I despise cleaning up Vadim's problems; I swore I wouldn't do it again. But here I am, on my way to parliament, because this damned country is on the verge of capsizing again, and I have to go twist arms to get a runoff vote. It's raining and the windows are getting fogged up on account of all this needless venting, but it's clear I have to tear the authority from my son's hands, take down *The Nation*'s entire editorial board, and ship the whole lot of them to uranium mining camps where they can quietly suffer the many accidents that happen to those who aren't careful.

I swear, it wasn't like this when I had power. It's embarrassing to expose this need to negotiate. In my day, I didn't negotiate with anyone. I didn't have to, because I had the foresight to avoid falling into these self-made traps that my son can't keep himself out of. I've seen this place from when it was first built, through six states of emergency, one civil war, innumerable victory parades. Young people today can't remember anything that didn't happen last month, and if you ask me this is why we have the problems we have today.

I can't start thinking like that right now. Otherwise, I'll take it out on an unsuspecting parliament. I should have stayed married long enough to have two sons, and that's my last word on the subject, I swear.

Let me give you a piece of advice. The moment you allow a little negligence into any system, you lose control of the whole thing. Chaos spreads like a fever dream. Once you lose control, you can never be seen convincingly as having it fully within your grasp again. Do you remember the TV show I had when I was president? Of course, as president people did love me, or at least they were expected to love me by law. With our only two channels airing my nightly two-hour address, they had little choice but to watch me and that was how I kept control of the big picture. Every night I was out there, explaining my perspective, leaving nothing to chance. Of course I could've been more cavalier back then. I was so self-serious when I was at my peak, bloated by the dreary delivery that comes with being in charge. Unless I was sternly interrogating a foreign spy captured by our intelligence agency, or testing the loyalty of a celebrity soccer player who'd failed to score a championship goal, my program was a nightly lecture about our national values as I prescribed them.

I gave myself to my people, every night for 29 years. I never wore the same suit twice. The six states of emergencies I delivered, as tanks rolled into the streets and snipers simultaneously took to the rooftops, are now studied as classics of political drama at Bleed University. If comedy wasn't my calling card, then I delivered gravitas in spades. I miss those days! After a full slate of presidential obligations, I would sit through two hours' worth of pre-production with scriptwriters, the first hour over catered dinners and the second in front of a mirror, having my sideburns combed and clipped, my wild eyebrows macheted like an unexplored jungle, then I'd power through two hours of on-air lectures, diatribes, and probing interviews, and only then did I allow myself to unwind a little.

I wrote the book on how to mix business and pleasure. Those legendary cognac sessions after each show, with my producers and an endless carousel of international celebrities, are never going to be part of the public record. Elite entertainment should never be on full display. It's the highlight of my presidential memory chest. Have you ever wrestled with the prince of Qatar after cognacs? When I stepped down, I gave Vadim my TV podium too. He neglected to see its value, cancelled it within a season.

Wait a moment. It seems we've come to a stop. I'm looking

out the window, and through that dense fog I get the impression we've been surrounded by black vans and motorcycles.

"What's going on?" I call to my chauffeur.

"Someone's blocked the road, sir."

"Lock the doors."

"Sir?"

"What is it?"

"There's a man with a machine gun knocking at my window. What do you want me to do?"

"I have one at my window too. Secure the doors, keep your hands useful. See what they want."

Vadim Bleed

I VAGUELY REMEMBER THE SKY outside going grey as I tucked into a course of seared Bluefin tuna steak caught in a mesh of onion confit and drowning in lentil purée. The chef was adamantly lecturing me on modern industry's rape of the oceans. I don't remember tasting the tuna at all, or any of the remaining courses. When I woke up, I was in bed, buried under a mound of pillows.

As I stumbled out of the bedroom, vaguely wondering how the floor knew not to light up in the daylight, I was surprised to find a man seated in the next room, his legs crossed, deeply absorbed with some reading material on a tablet. A handball tournament emanated from the flat screen. Before him on the coffee table were the remaining courses from last night's meal.

"You must be someone special if security let you in," I said.

"I am," he agreed. "Your friend Jojo sends his regards. I've been waiting for some time. Fortunately, there was a game on."

I looked him over: starched shirt, double-breasted blazer, flamboyant tube socks, a vaguely muscular *je ne sais quoi* of military hawkishness about him. "You're Russian, aren't you?"

He didn't deny this.

"Have you tasted these?" I gestured toward the food on the

coffee table. "This man is genius. I should offer him a job back home. Our chefs could learn a thing or two."

"I'm sure that's the case," he said. "Speaking of back home, I see you've had an election. We hope the results will fall in your favour."

"It's a formality. Due process."

"I've been doing a bit of reading about you." He tapped his tablet. "Sounds like you and your father aren't getting along. Should we be worried?"

"I don't know what you're talking about. We get along famously."

"This Transfusion blogger doesn't think so. It says here your men were fighting each other in the streets."

I took the tablet and looked over the article. "It's clickbait garbage. How can I be fighting my father while I'm here?"

"We understand family dynamics," he said. "We would like to see you resolve yours. I think we share your vision for the future of your country."

"What did you say your name was?"

"I haven't yet. In any case, it's not important in the grand scheme of things."

"You're interested in uranium then?"

"Sure. We think it's an important mineral in our future."

"Are you saying that as a potential customer or just an admirer?"

"Let's just say I'm another interlocutor, a facilitator. We like setting the right circumstances so that things flow naturally, of their own accord."

"That's beautiful. The land leases, as you surely know, are set to expire next year. Those who want to keep the status quo would rather I wasn't there when that moment comes. But there are others out there who, like me, would like to work out more mutually beneficial arrangements."

He smiled a little. "You're ambitious. I'll relay that to my people." He muted the handball match. "Our friends the Chinese are interested in securing a significant amount of uranium from a reliable and sustainable source. And for the right arrangement, they're willing to pay premium."

"The Allegory Mountains hold numerous deposits that have yet to be mined," I said. "Enough to keep an operation going for two generations. The Americans don't want us leasing those territories to others. But if there was some way to shake up that agreement…"

"Technology develops so quickly these days. Everyone in the market is researching new applications. I'm sure that territory is worth ten times what the Americans are offering you. Those who control the technology of tomorrow control, well, they control tomorrow."

"And you want the Chinese to control tomorrow," I finished his thought.

"Tell me, Mr. Bleed, are you content living in a world dominated by the Americans? Do you want to be stuck under all that weight when the balance of global power finally shifts away from the West? Ask yourself, do you want to be on the low rung of the wrong ladder in that scenario?"

"Of course not."

"The Americans provide you with jeeps and uniforms, low-level supplies. They care about their military interests, their multinational corporations, their bottom line, and regional stability. You're not on that list. They won't even talk to you. They send British ambassadors and CIA operatives dressed as mining officials to do their work."

"And you want to offer us a low rung on the right ladder."

"I'm offering you a chance to make the right alignment going forward. For your territory. For your bottom line."

"So why haven't you come to me before?"

"We're doing this everywhere. In fact, this offer is only on the table until we've met our quota in commitments, and then it's gone. You can either be part of the quota, or not."

"But you've waited a long time. The timing isn't great."

"Isn't it? Now, well, a lot of balls are up in the air. The election, the observers, the Lezers, the mining corporations, the intelligence community. Some balls could begin to drop in the next little while. That's bad for some and good for others. The natural order of things no longer applies and real change can break through."

"Let's suppose I agree in principle with everything you're saying."

"As Jojo said, it's better to be out of the picture when it all begins to unravel. People will look elsewhere for blame."

"But as leader, I get blamed for it all."

"That depends on the nature of the chaos."

"It sounds too complicated. It's a big risk for me to take. We're meeting in secret, no formal negotiations…"

"It's not often that an opportunity of this magnitude arrives to change a set course. We want to arrange the right circumstances for you so that the correct outcome flows from the natural order of events."

"If I were to take this course, when will the flow of events begin?"

"In our world, events are always flowing. Energy is wild and unpredictable. Think of your leadership, its force, as a river.

Where is your dam, Mr. Bleed? How can we help you find your true course?"

"Let's see what you can do."

"Everything will fall into place. And we'll be there at the end, ready to build a new future with you."

"Okay."

"Perfect." With that, the Russian who'd never bothered to introduce himself stood and left.

Mustafa Bleed

WHERE TO BEGIN? I'm inside the trunk of a car that's been lurching back and forth through the busy traffic of Qala Phratteh. We are, how to best put this, off script now. Excuse the whirring of the engine, the screeching of tires, the honking of horns, and the grunts and thumps of my body against the unforgiving interior. You have no way of telling, but I'm not as young and sculpted at 82 as my officially sanctioned, air-brushed public portraits would lead you to believe. When the car clips the corner of a sidewalk and my forehead hits the inside shaft of the trunk lid, it hurts.

Vadim Bleed

THE CAR HURTLED THROUGH the streets of central Vienna as Bruno unleashed an arsenal of friendly emojis to smooth over a potentially thorny exchange of text messages with the photo-shoot's producer. My meeting with the Russian being unscheduled, we were now running late!

"We're going to be all right," said Bruno. "The shoot is running late anyhow and they were worried we'd have to wait."

We finally screeched to a stop in front of an unmarked brick building deep in a questionable industrial neighbourhood, and I leapt out of the car to press the buzzer myself. A massive boulder of an Austrian skinhead pushed opened the steel door and nodded for us to enter. We followed this hulking figure down a poorly lit corridor into a freight elevator, which took us up four storeys and opened onto a spacious loft. A dour-looking dj in his 40s, spinning house music at a minimal volume, acknowledged our presence by pointing to a handwritten sign: he would not take requests. On the small dance floor, a petite redhead wearing only a man's undershirt and a bikini bottom swayed indifferently to the beat while deeply involved in a text she was composing. Beyond her, a small living room had been arranged, and several of the guest models were chattering forcefully around a generous hill of cocaine that the youngest son of Montenegro's president appeared to be divvying up with a platinum card. Along the back, the makeup artist, hairdresser, and costume designer had formed a beehive of cosmetic activity around the mostly naked ambassador from the Republic of Cabinda, a man I'd met at an alumni tennis tournament last year. From his riding boots and crop, I assumed they had an equestrian-themed montage in the works. Razoir, the trendy Viennese photographer known for his messy ambidextrous approach, was frantically flashing away with two cameras at once in the far corner, in search of the unpredictable angle that would produce the look of surprise he insisted upon. I couldn't see who he was shooting through the haze of dry ice. When a large snake slithered out of the haze, he called *Time!*, kicked a tripod out of his way in frustration, and stormed off the set. His assistant, an unassuming nineteen-year-old woman in cut-off jeans and a baseball cap, was left to track down the escaped reptile before it poisoned someone.

"Vadim Bleed!" Razoir called out as he walked toward my entourage with his arms in the air. After we kissed cheeks, he took me by the hand and led me to the living room. The other models, all ready for action in loose robes and bikini briefs, had just popped open a bottle of champagne when we arrived. The son of Montenegro's president, whose name I discovered is Dragaan, rose to offer me an overflowing flute.

"Would you like a touch-up?" He gestured to the coffee table covered in long lines of white dust that a muscled-up young man with a blond ponytail was sampling. I later learned that he was the grandson of a long-forgotten Governor General for Malta. "It's top-notch," Dragaan said.

"I don't know, boys," I said, not quite convincingly. "It's a long day." I looked around and saw that my entourage had melted away, as they'd been trained to do. Dignitaries don't appreciate hangers-on when in the presence of other dignitaries. I sat down, contemplating the mirrored coffee table.

"Because it's a long day," Razoir insisted.

"The snake's ready," the assistant called.

Razoir stood. "Listen, you get comfortable here, while I go finish up with those other two. Have a drink, relax in your own way. Don't worry about anything other than feeling beautiful for the camera. I'll call you when it's time."

The third man rolled a straw from an envelope-sized bill of some currency I didn't recognize and handed it to me. "Thanks," I said.

"Pascal," he said by way of introductions. "National Liberation Front of Corsica. We go together?" He gestured toward the table as if we were about to dive into a swimming pool.

"I'll race you," I replied. And so we dove in.

From that point on, we talked and snorted and talked some more and snorted some more, and generally I felt as though I was letting all the tension of the past week flow out of my mouth and into the attentive ears of the three models. The elections, the tragic earnestness of the opposition and aging parents, the merits of yoga, racing cars, horoscopes, palm readers. My opinions on these matters all sounded so lucid and well-articulated when I detailed them to people who, like me, lived with the pressures of all that great power and responsibility. By the time Razoir's assistant came looking for me, we'd drunk a lot of champagne, my mouth had gone numb, and I had made three new best friends.

"Good luck with everything!" They toasted me with shaky glasses.

Air-boxing with renewed confidence, I went off to makeup, hair and costuming feeling like a million of the Maltese liras we had just used as express elevators into our burning nostrils.

"Mind getting undressed?" said the makeup artist.

I stripped down.

"Jewellery too, please."

Gone.

As soon as the last toe-ring had been removed, she donned a surgical mask and spray-painted my entire body in a glittering fuchsia finish. After that, all three of them helped mount a majestic set of white-feathered wings onto my back, taking care to not smudge the still-glistening paint job around my shoulders.

"Am I a god?" I asked the costume designer. I stretched out my arms to get a fuller sense of my powerful wingspan.

"Razoir says you're an endangered species."

She pulled in a full-length mirror so I could get a better look.

"I better be the last of my kind," I said, satisfied.

Razoir signalled he was ready for me. I walked into the fog of dry ice and found myself attacked on all sides by bright flashes, until I no longer knew which way I was turning. I fell to the ground, stunned. Disoriented, barely able to see, my wings bent out of shape and my paint job perspiring away, I saw Razoir's legs walk into the haze. He stood over me and, with both arms outstretched, took two fatal shots. "Excellent," he mumbled under his breath. "You genuinely look damaged beyond repair."

"I hope it looks sexy," I said, nervous that it didn't.

"Sexy is boring," Razoir replied. "I'm a conjurer. I don't do sexy." Then he walked away and I was left with the queasy feeling that the snake was still hiding somewhere in the white smoke.

Mustafa Bleed

I'M A FORMER MILITARY MAN, special forces, so no, I'm not afraid. I'm too much of a prize for these idiots. Someone's made a rash decision, miscalculated that kidnapping me would tip Vadim's hand, and the country would change course out of some sentimental attachment. Of course, the General is going to crush whoever did this, whether it's New Nationalists or any one of their terrorist friends. Whoever did this has given us a window to wipe them all off the map. This is a gift.

As best as I can tell, I'm alone. In any case, no one has come through the door since I was installed here, in this room with no windows, only an old bureaucrat's desk, a creaking swivel chair and worn carpeting. It's been hours, I'm bored, a bit depressed, definitely hungry, maybe on the move, maybe not, for how long I have no clue.

Earlier today, as I was making my way to parliament, a masked gang cut off my car from the motorcade and shot my chauffeur and my security man. They did so knowing full well I was on my way to resolve this election mess. They shoved me into the back of the waiting van. It wove swiftly through the midday traffic, and soon we pulled into an underground parking lot. There, I was blindfolded before being led out the back. We walked for a short distance. I could hear the echo of our steps. There must've been at least four of us down there. I was guided into the trunk of another car. We drove around, oh, I don't know, less than an hour, long enough to feel every pothole and crack in Qala Phratteh's neglected streets, before pulling into another underground lot. I recognized the telltale descent, the never-ending turns. The trunk opened, I was helped out with some difficulty, led to an elevator, and taken up into what must have been an office building. By the time my blindfold was removed, I was alone in this sad office, this desk, this swivel chair, an ashtray, nothing more. I caught the back of a man leaving and locking the door behind him. I thought to myself, if they want something from me, this is where I'm going to be interrogated. But that hasn't happened yet, which leads me to believe that this is less about me, and more about what I could mean to someone else. I began to wonder if there was a price on my head, and how much, in general, I could be worth in such a situation. Pragmatically speaking, I'm a prize.

It must be dark out now. The boredom I can handle, but not knowing what's next or who's in charge of this little escapade, that's a bit tougher to stomach. My bones start to hurt whenever I miss my afternoon nap. When I miss a meal the acids in my stomach become temperamental and boil up into my chest. My most pressing concern: I have medications that need to be taken like clockwork; I'm like the engine of a car that requires a regular oil change. If I go too far without a refill from my rainbow of pills, panic lights start flashing all across the dashboard of my mind.

Vadim Bleed

LATE INTO THE NIGHT, as we danced among the predatory third wives of old Viennese leather barons in the VIP room of an east-end swingers' club, I pulled aside the Corsican nationalist at the bar, ordered us two more dirty martinis, and slurred a question I'd been obsessing over since that moment Razoir stepped away and left me in the fog. "Do you feel endangered?" I asked.

"I think we'll be all right here," he replied, looking back at the roomful of experienced spouses and spies gyrating to the chorus of a perverted cabaret singer. "It's a thrill just to be here for most of these people. But they won't do much harm."

"I mean as a leader. I wonder sometimes how possible it is, anymore, to make a real difference. The rules have grown so complex, the world so interconnected. So many people outside your own borders feel as though you owe them."

"My job – your job," he said, tapping me on the chest, "is to keep the idea of purity alive, to be a principle, a standard. My goal is to articulate a vision of the Corsican future, to be uncompromising in the face of all that impossibility that exists in its way. I am the Corsica-in-waiting for Corsicans when they feel the world hasn't done enough for them. That feeling is more prevalent than ever. Global this, international that. The average person has never felt so small. It's better if people think I'm endangered. It keeps me alive."

"That's what I want, Pascal," I said. Without looking back, I discreetly pushed away a mysterious tongue that was licking my ear. "I want to feel necessary."

"You're a leader. Be it."

"It's complicated. I'm the third president in my family line. The pose is too familiar," I confessed. "I take it all in stride, I'm not a stressed-out person, but do you know how hard it is to compete against the entire history of your country? My grandfather, who was president for 17 years, named the place. My father was president for 29 years. And now I have to deal with globalization of all things."

"You're a corrupted principle," Pascal said. "An idea and the power to fulfill it are two very different things."

I was about to disagree with him outright, but he'd already dispensed two little mounds of cocaine on a silver cigarette case, and by the time we'd each taken our turn I thought there had been some hard truth in what he said. "Let's be honest," I said, "the problem is that it's damn near impossible to be a powerful person these days. Constant work. No respect. Everybody wants to use you, and nobody wants to listen to you. You have enemies everywhere. Everyone, regardless of how uneducated they are, feels they have the right to shit on you in any bar in the world. It's enough to make you want to quit, Pascal."

"So quit," he said. "Didn't you say you'd just had an election? Let the other side have a go. Let them see how it will wear them down."

Our drinks arrived and we had a brief argument over who would pick up the tab, which devolved to pulling out our wallets and throwing competing credit cards on the bar before an intimidated bartender. I ended up buying drinks for everyone.

My mobile buzzed in my pocket. I shot back my dirty martini, excused myself, and walked toward the patio to take the call. Outside, the night air was refreshing compared to the humidity of the club. It was Zaan. "Yes?" I said by way of answering.

"Where are you?" he said with urgency. "Are you safe?"

I looked around and saw only a man my father's age in a leather jumpsuit, giving me eyes. "Relatively," I said.

"Mighty Mouse has been kidnapped."

"For fuck's sake, as if we need more to deal with right now. What do they want? Ransom?"

"There's no claim. It's all…"

I heard gunfire, and then the sound of rapid footsteps. "Hold on, I can't hear you. Are you running?"

"His men think it's us. They think it's you. We're under attack."

I heard more clack-clacking of machine guns, and then a deep grunt. And then it sounded like Zaan's phone hit the ground. I could hear footsteps approaching and then faintly, someone saying, *Get his mobile.* I hung up and looked around with new eyes, feeling deeply exposed. I tried not to appear nervous. To counteract the rising tide of stress in my chest, I struck up a conversation with the man in the leather jumpsuit and managed to bum a cigarillo while warding off his advances.

This wasn't good. My number was on that phone.

I puffed away fiercely at my cigarillo, and that last martini began to swim electric laps in the pool of my charged thoughts. A little chaos would catch everyone off guard. Let them react, let them make mistakes. Let them guess who's thinking what. London School of Economics, baby. Let us help you, Vadim, when the moment is right. But this was turning into a lot of chaos. From the ledge of the tall building, Vienna lit up with a thousand bright lights below. My hands shook with excitement as I discreetly tossed my phone into the abyss. A moment later, I heard the sound of a car alarm.

Who Would Kidnap Mustafa Bleed?

by Kaarina Faasol

As some of you are well aware by now, the 82-year-old strongman Mustafa Bleed was kidnapped yesterday in a highly coordinated attack on his motorcade. He was headed to the Parliament building, where he was expected to make an important announcement regarding the election results, which have yet to be made public.

No matter who is responsible, the kidnapping constitutes the biggest blow to the Bleed government since the assassination of Blanco Bleed in 1979. But some here are wondering how the attack could have penetrated and dismantled the ex-president's security detail with such sharply executed efficiency, at a time of heightened security. No one in President Bleed's administration has commented publicly on this development that has stunned officials across the region.

The events of the day are still unclear, but a piecemeal version of what happened is emerging through a survey of witnesses and through conversations with government insiders who cannot speak on the record, due to the sensitivity of the situation. The entire attack, I'm told, took less than three minutes. More than 20 masked gunmen were involved, a conspicuously large group to go under the radar for long.

Inside the Bleed government, I'm told by my sources within the Ministry of Information, senior officials are already pointing fingers at a web of Lezer militias in the restive northwest region where the Allegory Mountains straddle the border. There's talk of a growing case that ties these militias to NNP candidate Fatma Gavras. Apparently, a mother of four intended to blackmail the Bleed government into opening the vote tabulation to an outside audit.

"I find that hard to swallow," said Gavras when I described the story being circulated. "I can't see how someone working from the outside would be able to pull off such a major operation. There are classified schedules to know in advance, knowledge of routes, and heavy security to contend with. And then there's the fact that it's Mustafa Bleed."

Gavras smells an inside job, but it's impossible to tell at this early juncture. She can't rule out other factions, "but no one else would have the access and resources to pull this off. This sets our efforts back. We're already being watched, so how could something so desperate and doomed to failure come to happen from our camp?"

The timing of the accusation is convenient for Vadim Bleed. He doesn't want his father in the picture, he does need a scapegoat to blame for getting rid of him, and wouldn't it all fit into place perfectly if that scapegoat were threatening to upend his election win and his family's legacy. "I don't know Vadim Bleed personally," says Gavras when I ask her about my pet theory, "but I have heard that he's unpredictable. I know he and his father don't see eye to eye, but I wouldn't think it could get this out of hand between them. But I honestly don't know."

One person who might know is New Nationalists leader Dabny Bolshoi. "The timing is suspect, you're right," he says, "but who's behind it is irrelevant at the moment. We're no longer having a conversation about possibly defeating the Bleeds at the polls. Instead, the conversation has shifted to treason or some other incitement to civil war. And now we have to worry for our lives instead of our votes."

Whatever the case may be, this writer pledges to get to the bottom of this seismic moment in our nation's politics. More to come as this story develops.

Mustafa Bleed

I ASK YOU AGAIN: what's a father to do when all his remaining options are bad? I'd fallen asleep on the floor, military style, using my blazer as a makeshift pillow, with this one thought in my head. I'd slept hard, fending off disturbing dreams, probably to do with cravings for the medications. It must've been well into the night when the door finally opened. A gorilla mask poked me in the ribs with the butt end of his Kalashnikov.

"Get up," he commanded. "We're leaving."

"Tell me, who do you work for?" I asked, expecting the masked man would recognize me, and that my engagement would be enough to intimidate him. "You can still save yourself."

The gorilla said nothing, or was under instructions to say nothing, perhaps advised of my uncanny ability to negotiate myself out of tight scenarios – the Houdini of hostage negotiations the French newspaper *Le Monde* had once called me in the '70s. He was no one important, not driving this plan, just there to blindfold me again and lead me down to the garage.

Instead of delivering me to the backseat of the waiting car as I hoped, he once again directed me into the trunk, where I now find myself. Just moments ago, the car stopped and I heard sheep bleating, the pestering calls of a shepherd. It must be dawn out there. How I miss the ability to read the sky. I could almost feel the brush of sheep's wool against the sides of the car, as if they were sidling up to my own skin.

These kinds of spontaneous diversions from my routine – it's very important that I keep on schedule these days – get under my skin. Even if this is the work of the opposition, I have only Vadim to blame. In five short years, his feeble attention span has emboldened Bolshoi and his gang of bohemian, tea-sipping chess players, whom I alternately entertained and arrested for nearly three decades. Now look what happens: that puppet opposition, whom I'd merely paid off as sequestered sparring partners to sharpen my debating skills, have the gall to bang their fists in frustration. I'm in the trunk of this car, when it should be my son.

Seven nights ago, when my intelligence attachés arrived to suggest plans for exile in the event that Vadim lost, I paid them no attention – I never lose. But now I'm second-guessing myself. It's all a big mess, I'm afraid.

I miss my father, the way we respected each other, stood side by side. My father Blanco gave me a free country, one he'd negotiated out of British imperialist quicksand and fussed over like a delicate rose for its first 17 years. I often referred to him as The Original on my nightly program. I loved and revered him, so unlike my son who has no respect for me.

The night before the election, I spent the evening with the General. The General and I, we'd had more than our fair share of cognacs, and as morning set in we realized with great sadness that the day we'd been avoiding had finally come. We could no longer postpone this botched election, not after the downtown riot, not after the staged bombing near the embassy district. That morning after the sun rose, people would begin streaming out of their homes to cast their ballots. We knew that no amount of intimidation – no roving jeeps of cocaine-fuelled rookie soldiers prowling city streets off-leash, no middle-of-the-night arrests of the opposition leader's cousin – would stop people from voting against my son. Even to us, at that hour, the prospect of Vadim guiding us through another five years, given the efforts we'd put forward to massage a win for him, seemed grave for the country and our family.

"What can a father do?" I complained. "I can't simply remove him from his post. It would look like I was scolding him in public, sending him to his room."

The General leaned forward with interest and nodded in agreement. It was the first time I'd been so frank about my misgivings with Vadim's presidency, and I knew he felt as dissatisfied as I did. It was then I gave him a look we both understood to mean that I was granting him a rare opportunity to speak candidly, that I was out of rope and could use the insights of someone who had been a frequent collaborator in both matters of discretionary, personalized arrests and mass public suppressions. I prefer, at all other times, to talk only in platitudes and veiled symbolism about my family affairs with anyone who is not a Bleed. It's beneath us to gossip about it. We are a liberation family, as close to royalty as you can get in this country. And so the General mulled over his every word as cautiously as if he were walking through a minefield.

"You have this double responsibility, to your family's legacy and to the nation's people."

"They're all my children," I agreed, examining his eyes for a sense of where he was heading with his thought.

"With the right conditions, you could still play a hand." He was kneading his knuckles as if he didn't know how to broach the delicate subject. "You must think about your legacy first and foremost, not just your family's."

"The Bleeds have protected the liberation for half a century," I reminded him. "After all this time, we can't just give the country away to Bolshoi. It's only a matter of time before he flushes it all away."

"Which do you want more? To keep the opposition out of power, or to keep your disappointment from getting aired in public?"

"I am my son," I said. "He's my responsibility. To have him lose everything would be the same as me letting down my own father. I'm in a bind."

He sat back and sighed. "I'm with you till the end."

As the car makes a sharp turn, I'm jolted back to the blackness inside the trunk. After a slow and winding drive down a bumpy country road, we appear to have stopped. I hear footsteps and a muffled conversation outside. Funny how events only seem relevant in the right context. I hadn't thought much of that late-night cognac ramble since it happened, but when the trunk finally swung open, it was the first thing to flood back into my thoughts.

PART 2

COMPLICATIONS

THE NATION

MAHBAD'S NEWS SOURCE SINCE 1964

State of Emergency Declared

Elections results to be withheld indefinitely

BY NADA FERBER

The Ministry of the Interior declared a nationwide state of emergency yesterday following the kidnapping of former president Mustafa Bleed.

Until further notice, all non-essential government services have been suspended. Citizens are advised to stay indoors except for emergencies or basic necessities. Businesses have been ordered to limit their hours of operation. The military will arrest anyone on the streets after 8 p.m.

Clashes between anti-Bleed protesters and government forces intensified across Qala Phratteh last night as a wave of kidnappings gripped the countryside.

"With the brazen kidnapping of one of our country's most cherished founders, the militant forces of this country's opposition have ventured dangerously into unprecedented territory," said General Constantin Benini at a press briefing.

Election results will now be withheld indefinitely, the General's statement confirms, for fear they could be used as a bargaining chip by either side. The statement does not rule out that the contested results could be thrown out altogether in favour of a new election, if the current crisis escalates.

Wary of the distrust that Mustafa Bleed's kidnapping could provoke, Dabny Bolshoi of the New Nationalists Party went out of his way, uncharacteristically, to support the military's decision to impose a state of emergency. He urged his party's membership to respect the curfew and stay off the streets for the time being.

However, NNP deputy leader Fatma Gavras has opted to defy Bolshoi's advice, calling for her followers to continue demonstrations and not give in to what she described as more government interference.

"The Bleeds will do anything to maintain the way of life from which they benefit and from which the rest of us suffer," Gavras wrote in a statement being circulated among NNP supporters.

"Let us not forget that changing the course of our future after 50 years of dictatorship was never going to be handed to us with an election victory. The election results were always going to be the beginning of a larger struggle. Our votes' disappearance is the surest signal we have of winning."

Sources close to the NNP leaders have noted that tensions are running high behind the scenes. Bolshoi has suspicions that one of the Gavras-affiliated armed militias is behind the ex-president's kidnapping. For her part, Gavras has begun to openly question Bolshoi's commitment to progress after years of collaborating with the current regime.

Long-time allies of Bolshoi, a 30-year veteran of Bleed's "faithful opposition," have said the elder statesman has been chafing at the apparent popularity of his new public counterpart. Some say Bolshoi and Gavras have recently argued over the direction of the coalition.

SUMCAX, the conglomerate of foreign-owned uranium companies, has issued its own statement calling for calm. "The industry needs a reliable negotiating partner at the country's helm, the group notes. Any prolonged power struggle will put pressure on already sceptical investors to think twice about pouring more resources into the region."

President Vadim Bleed remains out of the country. He is said to be weighing security options for his return with a small circle of advisors.

Mustafa Bleed

AT FIRST, I COULDN'T see anything. My eyes had grown accustomed to the crowded black shadows of that trunk, the jagged rocking of mountain roads, and when the trunk finally popped open, I was caught lying on my back with both arms and legs pressed to the sides of the cab, as I'd learned way back in my military training, squinting into a bright ceiling of sudden daylight. It took several seconds to finally focus on the General's dark silhouette standing there, his hand extended. Someone else could have shot me twice in the chest in that time. Weakly, I grabbed his forearm and let him help me to my feet.

"No one tells me anything anymore," I complained. "What are you up to?"

"I'm being creative." He looked me over. "Are you hurt?"

"I've survived worse." I brushed off my suit, straightened my tie, and adjusted my cuffs.

"Good, follow me."

For the first time, I looked around. We were in the circular driveway of the old British Embassy Retreat, an abandoned weekend resort in the Allegory Mountains beyond Qala Phratteh that was once frequented by foreign diplomats and their vacationing families. These days, the military and secret police were its only visitors. Officially, no one had been allowed past those rusting iron gates since the British left.

"You're not going to murder me, are you?" I was joking, but only half so.

"Not at all," the General said as we walked up the stone stairs to the front doors of the main building. From the front doors of the Retreat, we could see the full expanse of rolling hills, flush with dark cedars all the way down to Qala Phratteh.

"When I was a boy," I said as we stood out there, "before independence, my father used to bring me up here for his meetings. I remember they had a family of kangaroos from Australia living on these grounds. That was the story. I'd spend all my time walking through the forests out back, looking for them. I never found them."

"It's still a rumour that pops up here and there," the General said. "Every once in a while, one of the men hears something rustling in the night."

"Am I under arrest? Who are you working for?"

"Nothing's changed. I've always worked for you, and I will always work for you."

"And so you kidnapped me right before a crucial speech to parliament?"

"I didn't kidnap anybody. In fact," he gestured to the city down in the valley, "I'm still down there looking for you."

"When will I reappear?"

"When the time's right. Until then, you'll be safe and comfortable with us. Think of it as a vacation. Come inside."

With his hairy hand on my back, guiding me in a friendly

but firm way, the General led me inside the humid central lobby of the old resort. Before us, a pair of grand staircases curved upward in opposite directions.

"I haven't stood here in front of these stairs since I was 13 years old," I said, looking up.

"We had an elevator installed some time ago."

He motioned behind the stairs. We took the small elevator to the second floor, a journey that took almost as long as the stairs would have. Once there, we stepped out into a hallway that stretched out in both directions. Closed doors lined each side, and it appeared we were the only people in the building.

"Where is everyone? We can't possibly be the only ones here."

The General ignored my question and began to walk down the corridor. "Listen, Mustafa, we're about to let things get messy. Think of it as a reset button."

"If you play with fire, it can burn you too."

"Sadly, this is the only option we have now," he said matter-of-factly. "You'll be the ultimate winner, but there have to be a few moves in between here and the new normal. Our window of opportunity is only open for a short while if this is to work."

"Does Vadim know what you're doing?"

"No one knows what they don't need to know. This has thrown both sides off guard. Our people in parliament believe the opposition is to blame. They're eager to use this to cover up the election. New Nationalists, they're going through their people to find out if anyone did this on their own. And if they do have you, then they want to know how much bargaining power this gives them to pry loose the results. We can expect violent demonstrations, kidnappings, people taking matters into their own hands all across the country. Someone will have to step in and take power before the whole place falls apart."

"It takes so long to build," I said. My head hurt. "How demoralizing to watch it crumble so quickly."

"A controlled demolition," he corrected. "The military, Mustafa, we're the only ones whose hands are not tainted in all this. We have to create the opportunity from which people can accept us taking back power. From there, we can find a way forward. Move Vadim into exile, where he practically lives anyways. Push hard on Bolshoi, cut his people back down to size. Once things settle, we release you, arrest anyone who's a threat. The military sets a date for elections six months down the road. We ask you, kidnapped hero to the people, to step in as interim leader, to have the wisdom of your guiding hand."

"I would decline. I can't be seen as taking my son's place like this."

"Sure. You could decline at first. But after more trouble in the streets, a few deaths, some protests calling for order, we would ask you again to lead us, only temporarily, through the storm. After that, calm would prevail, life would return to normal, and a second election would be yours to win."

"Or postpone," I laughed nervously.

He joined me, which lightened the mood considerably. "This shouldn't be any different than 1983."

We reminisced about the events of 1983. The General and I had been through a lot together. I had to admit, for all the anxiety and bruising I'd suffered, it was a good plan.

Vadim Bleed

I WON'T LIE TO YOU: I'm a little spooked by everything that's going on. So I've decided to leave my private plane and my entourage behind, strike out on my own, purchase a Porsche and drive, go off grid, simply disappear for a while and hide out in the unpredictable hinterlands of my imagination until this whole mess sorts itself out. I sped my new cruiser out of the Viennese luxury-car dealership, along the cobblestone streets of the old city, sending a carriage horse or two lurching back onto their hind legs, and fled toward the Austrian wilderness like a hunted fox.

For hours I drove and drove, and as I approached the Central Eastern Alps, low-hanging clouds pressed down closer and the blur of grassy knolls and evergreens turned white with snow.

As if to ruin it all, one of my mobiles rang. Fuck me, I thought, looking up out the window to make sure there wasn't a drone above waiting to fire as soon as I answered. I answered and heard the General's concerned voice on the other end.

"Tell me, how are you enjoying yourself?" he asked.

"It's been a good trip. Productive. How are things back home?"

"Seems you've got yourself into some trouble. Maybe you're talking too freely."

"I don't know what you're referring to."

"Oh, I don't want the back and forth. We have recordings for that. I'm more interested in context. Do you know who you were talking to?"

"An associate of an old friend from university days. I didn't catch his name."

"You didn't catch his name because he's former KGB. Let me share a little something with you. We captured the men who kidnapped your father."

"Oh, splendid. Lezer terrorists?"

The line went quiet for a moment. "Mostly Lezers, yes. But a few had Chechen backgrounds."

"What do Chechens have to do with anything?"

"Well, these ones have a history of working for the KGB."

"You're saying I had something to do with the kidnapping?"

"Your father's prospects grow dimmer the longer he's out there. He's an old man with many needs."

"I don't know if that's an update or a threat."

"I don't know either. Given how poorly these elections have gone, maybe for you it's an opportunity."

"I think my father rigged this election so that I would lose. To humiliate me. I don't think any of you are on my side."

"Don't get paranoid."

"Why not? I'm boxed in a corner. Maybe I'm better off with outside help, working with people who don't share your interests."

Here he laughed a little. "I see. You're looking ahead."

"I've been left with no other choice."

The signal died, and I realized that all that time I'd been

driving on instinct, not really paying attention to where I was going. My Porsche and I were among mountains on all sides, winding along a wet road on a grey afternoon as a light snow fell on my windshield and melted away. As I drove through a valley and up the side of a mountain, with its tightening bends and narrowing road, I thought about those Conflict Management courses again, that game-theorist professor who I'd once found so dry. Look what he'd done for me now. I would've never considered kidnapping my pa for show, but now that I have I can use that for internal leverage.

An hour passed and the terrain grew more rugged. It began to snow harder as the sky darkened. I had to give my all to the challenge of navigating the low-riding, rear-wheel-drive sports vehicle. I turned on my high beams and leaned forward to navigate the increasingly treacherous road. The Porsche kept lurching forward, its wheels spinning. Up ahead I spotted a blue sign through the slanting snow: Slovakia 5 km.

TRANSFUSION BLOG

A Brief History of Bleed Country

by Kaarina Faasol

International readers have started to write me, which is heartening. Often, they ask how the Bleeds came to power. Chances are, if you live outside our borders, you don't know much about our nation's turmoil, because any attempt to make it known officially has been stamped out or sanded over by the Bleed government. What is the backstory for this election, they ask; how are we supposed to view it?

We are nowhere near the Western world; we don't have much strategic value, apart from our uranium deposits. The mining conglomerates are happy to keep it that way too. Those massive quarries deep in the Allegory Mountains are at the centre of why our politics have gone so off track over the decades.

Ours is a tiny territory, a backyard province of the Ottoman Empire that later ended up an obscure British colony until 1961. The official story goes that Blanco Bleed – Mustafa's father, Vadim's grandfather – single-handedly negotiated an independence treaty for his people when the British began finding it too expensive to maintain the region. What is more often forgotten is that Blanco was effectively crowned our first president. As one of our few foreign-educated elites of that time, he was spearheading the uranium-mining developments in the Allegory Mountains that the British were reluctant to leave behind.

Also erased from the official history by successive Bleeds is the fact that Blanco had strong competition for the job of "chief administrator for the mines" – this was the wording the British used to describe the presidency in their exit plans. Alman Bentrogliu, then a prominent voice in the Lezer community, was also lobbying the departing colonists for the new nation's leading post, but ultimately he was seen as being too untrustworthy with the mining portfolio. Back in the '50s, his Lezer community represented 57% of the region's population.

These are the beginnings of the tragic Boran-Lezer sectarian divide that continues to plague our nation to this day. With the presidency in hand and his British supervisors otherwise distracted by the clearance sale of their global empire, Blanco Bleed began using his powers to divert all manner of privileges to his Boran peoples, claiming to be only righting a historical imbalance. But what first began as a matter of improving schools in the Boran regions soon grew into the purging of Lezers from the old British-directed government bureaucracy and the appointing of a generation of nationalist Boran judges to our highest courts.

Bentrogliu, who became something of a cult celebrity in international politics throughout the '60s, fought Blanco Bleed all the way to the United Nations, where he famously addressed the assembly of nations with his tribal dagger in hand. That was in 1973. By 1974 he was dead, the victim of a plane crash off the coast of Majorca. An investigation eventually deemed the cause of the crash to be mechanical failure, but by then a Bleed conspiracy had already formed in the minds of many Lezers. In 1979, Blanco Bleed was assassinated by a student during a graduation ceremony.

Mustafa Bleed, who succeeded his father in the fog of national mourning, was voted into power behind closed doors by a national parliament composed of Blanco Bleed henchmen. Opposition to that travesty of justice was fierce across the nation. To stamp it out, Mustafa ruled with a big-stick mentality from the start, setting loose largely Boran police forces on demonstrators who opposed him and instigating a clandestine network of informers that often saw his opponents kidnapped and tortured.

Amidst this poisonous climate, his 1983 re-election campaign devolved into a 16-month civil war, followed by three more years of political purging, that saw Bleed's Boran government murder more than 26,000 Lezers and push another 73,000 into exile. Along the way, Bentrogliu's old Independence United party was deemed illegal and dismantled, replaced by the Bleed-curated New Nationalists Party, led by a servile former Bleed bureaucrat named Dabny Bolshoi.

Among those 26,000 killed was the father of Lezer parlia-mentarian Fatma Gavras. Gavras herself was a 22-year-old mother of two young daughters when Mustafa Bleed first took over. By the time he finally ceded power in 2008, she was 51, already a grandmother of six and a doctor with a reputation for helping the poor. Because she's a Lezer and has a reputation for speaking her mind, Gavras is branded a radical.

She first met Dabny Bolshoi during the 2008 campaign, when the veteran politician approached the doctor to run for parliament in her district. The New Nationalists Party thought that she would do well. Though she won her seat, the overall 2008 winner was yet another Bleed, 32-year-old Vadim, best known as a tabloid celebrity who hosted beauty pageants and raced cars.

Today, many people know Dabny Bolshoi as the wronged presidential candidate, a stifled agent of change. And this is true, in part. Many insiders say that decades of leading the nation's only sanctioned opposition group has left Bol-shoi feeling alienated and hungry for change in his old age. The past five years of neglect under Vadim Bleed have only added insult to injury.

Just days ago, Bolshoi was ready to give the election away. Despite the United Nations' claim that New Nationalists won at the polls, the military elite that operates in the shadows behind the Bleeds asked Bolshoi to reconsider claiming the win in order to avoid another civil war. Faced with this stark reality – and threats to his family – Bolshoi began negotiating a way out with the regime.

Against her boss's warnings, Fatma Gavras has continued to take to the streets in frustration. She's grown into the unlikely face of a national movement that could provoke change in a country whose opposition has been fragmented and whose citizens have been oppressed for half a century. The protests proved to be an unexpected wrench in Bolshoi's plans.

Since then, the country has spiraled into chaos. The nightly demonstrations grew faster than even Gavras could have anticipated. Mustafa Bleed has been kidnapped, and Vadim Bleed is hiding somewhere outside the country. The military has imposed a state of emergency, and the results from the election have been shelved indefinitely.

Raising her voice hasn't come without consequences for Gavras. The police have shown up at her home in the middle of the night, claiming to have search warrants. Two days ago, a car exploded outside her door. She's had to send her family away, because she can't guarantee their safety any longer.

For the moment, Gavras has the people on her side, though that support may recede as the country hurtles quickly toward the unknown. She also appears to have the tacit support of Western governments who've been watching from a distance. UK ambassador Louise Pressinger called Gavras's movement "potentially the most important grassroots development the country has seen since Independence United's Alman Bentrogliu." Whether or not Gavras wants to wear that crown of thorns remains to be seen.

Mustafa Bleed

THE GENERAL HAS ARRANGED makeshift living quarters for me on the second floor of the British Retreat, in a disused gallery. The walls are still haunted by the ghosts of the paintings that once hung here. At the end of this long and echoladen room I've discovered a grand piano beneath a large white sheet. But no one has come to play it for me yet. There are six French doors that have yet to let in a single ray of sunlight. The long balcony where I now stand, waiting for the fog of my unmedicated thoughts to dissipate in the fresh mountain air, is splattered with bird shit and dead leaves.

I slept badly last night.

Come, help me over to the railing and let me give you a history lesson, to put some of the past few days in perspective. See over those trees, that long stretch of tarmac to the north of the city, with those low, long buildings? That's Bleed International Airport, one of the many jewels of my dear Blanco's legacy. It opened in 1972 to great fanfare. We had many international journalists on hand, all writing articles on how a visit to our new country should be on every global adventurer's itinerary, with little bits about our five-star hotel, our archaeological digs, our casinos. The grand opening of the new airport and the cutting of the ribbon for our new airline had been the twin pinnacles of my father's vision for this country. Ten years earlier, when he'd claimed our independence from the British, he nationalized those vast uranium mines, and the profits of those dealings bought him an airline. Later, I had to re-mortgage those very mines to the Americans in exchange for the aid our military needed to buy arms and intelligence, to put down the Lezer uprisings, which is why it was so vital for Vadim to regain them for us, to respect my father's vision.

For weeks leading up to the grand unveiling of his dream, Blanco would drive around Qala Phratteh, telling anyone who would listen that their country would soon have the clout of a Switzerland or Lebanon. It meant a lot to him. So what does Alman Bentrogliu do? He blows up an outgoing flight seconds after it leaves the runway. It came hurtling down in a ball of flames right in those mountains there, caused a huge forest fire, killed all 187 passengers onboard, and destroyed our image in the eyes of the world. Seven international airlines cancelled their stops here. Eight years of work, gone, in a day.

Now, follow my finger to the west. See that giant radio tower there, at the base of the mountains? That's the old signal tower for the now-defunct Independence United radio station. Alman Bentrogliu launched his station in 1965 after he lost his first election to my father. It was from there that Alman announced that *The Nation*, our newspaper, was nothing more than a governmental applause line used to force through everything from new traffic lights to trade treaties with the British. To appease him, my father set it up as an independent entity. He accused our military of being propped up by British intelligence. My father had the British pull back their operatives from public view. He accused my mother of having British blood in her family. When Alman Bentrogliu lost the 1969 elections, he came out and accused my father of rigging the vote. It never ended.

See the low hills to the right of the station? Behind there is where Alman Bentrogliu began assembling a Lezer militia that year, the Independence United Army. He riled up hate in every last one of them. Before Alman, the Lezers couldn't care less who was administering their roads or boiling their water so long as they were left alone and could visit relatives across the border without anyone holding them up. The militia dug tunnels all through those mountains. We joke that the Allegory Mountains earned their mythic name because there wasn't much of the mountains left after they had dug so many tunnels in them. That's when the explosions began. First a grocery store, then a movie theatre, a restaurant, a mineshaft. Then the bombing at the airport, then hijackings.

I was 42 at the time, an elder statesman of the Greco-Roman wrestling world. My father had given me a diplomatic appointment some years before, to groom me for government life because I suppose you could say I was a little lost then, like Vadim is now. I hadn't done much travelling since the Munich Olympics, where the final gold medal of my athletic career had been upstaged by a hostage-taking, so I decided it would be best to go abroad for a while and tour the world. I drove down to the Mediterranean coast and set off by yacht from there, with only a minimal staff. It's fair to say I was feeling out of focus.

For three months I had little contact with the outside world, other than the week I spent at an old wrestling friend's vacation home on Santorini. Each night he and I traded shots of ouzo and forkfuls of octopus on his white rooftop, all the while complaining about our hijacking epidemic, which had captivated the world's attention for all the wrong reasons. They were an infestation on our airline, mangling our otherwise profitable money-laundering clientele and skyrocketing the costs of insuring our fleet of airplanes. The question of what to do about it was being held up in our divisive parliament, where the hijackers had the support of, you guessed correctly, Alman Bentrogliu and Independence United parliamentarians.

Upon my return home, I could plainly see that my father's troubles had worn him down. His hair had thinned and greyed. He had dark craters under his eyes. His wilting dreams kept him from sleeping at night. His chauffeur and private secretary both complained to me that he'd grown suspicious and irritable. The airport and national airline he'd once hoped would elevate us in the eyes of the world had instead transformed the country into a free-for-all for hijackers and anarchists. The passion that I'd always discerned in his eyes was no longer there.

I've had something on my mind ever since the General brought me here: I had Alman Bentrogliu assassinated. I never told my father or anyone else. I had to make it look like an accident, to avoid anyone pointing fingers at my family. I knew that Alman Bentrogliu, apart from being a staunch nationalist, was also a lover of classical music and something of an amateur-rank composer from his more bohemian days. In fact, his wife was the first-chair clarinetist in our fledgling National Symphony Orchestra. He had even composed our national anthem. Whenever possible, he would travel with the orchestra to see her perform. It was his secretive way of meeting with the foreign sympathizers who bankrolled him – we knew that. These trips happened six or seven times a year, mostly as part of an orchestra exchange program with other small countries of the world. So they were off to Luxembourg or Andorra or Albania, and we would receive whatever the other country sent our way.

On November 26th, 1974, as our National Symphony Orchestra and their spouses flew to the Canary Islands, their plane disappeared somewhere over the Mediterranean Sea. Majorcan search crews scoured the waters near the pilot's last radio transmission, but no survivors were found. The worst was confirmed four days later, when beachgoers in Barcelona found an errant violin bow washed up on the shore during morning tide. The Canary Island musicians, flabbergasted at the fate of their cultural counterparts and wanting somehow to console our people, offered to perform as part of the state funeral procession that wound through Qala Phratteh two days later. They were the most mournful steel-drum troupe any of us had ever heard.

The country did improve. The era of hijackings eventually came to an end. Then in 1979, on the fifth anniversary of Alman's death, my father was assassinated. He'd been invited to give a speech to the graduating class at Bleed University, and as his new Minister of Sport and Education, I accompanied him to the university that morning and was sitting in the audience while he spoke onstage. A student only six or seven rows from the front stood up during the address. I recall thinking, *Where's he going in the middle of the ceremony?* Because of his black robe and where he was positioned in the auditorium, I couldn't see what he was reaching for, but by the time his arm was outstretched and he was firing off, it was too late. That student only had seconds before my father's security shot him dead. But it was long enough.

In the back of a speeding Mercedes-Benz, I held my father in my arms as he grew colder. I watched him go pale and trail away. We sat in the back of the car, not uttering a single word as it wove through midmorning traffic to the hospital. His blood, which was also my blood, seeped onto the leather upholstery and into the shoulder of my blazer.

To this day, the country still mourns the deaths of its founding father and first opposition leader, which I enshrined as an official holiday in 1980 during my second year as president. In a speech to tens of thousands gathered at Revolution Square, I declared the past firmly behind us. Moving forward, we would leave behind the vengeful ways of previous generations and start fresh. Then came the Lezer uprisings, the '83 civil war, the formation of New Nationalists... There was so much to do, always. I never looked back.

Vadim Bleed

THERE ARE PLACES WHERE YOU ought to think hard about whether it's wise to push a brand-new performance vehicle to its limits. The neglected mountain roads that thread the Western Carpathian Mountains, I can now confirm, are one of those places. Several reasons. Firstly, the wet snows of spring can get thick once daylight disappears. Secondly, those humps and puddles cratering the road hurt that much more when you can't see them coming. Thirdly, long car trips on little sleep have a way of lulling my thoughts. My body shifts to autopilot while the mind drifts along an even more treacherous race course of traumatizing memories. I should slow down, I realized finally, when it was really too late to do anything about it. The car had already slid out from under me at that point and was spinning helplessly toward a knot of virgin beech trees. I braced for the impact, momentarily airborne, slammed into a tree trunk with a groan, sliding down into a muddy ditch beside the road. An ancient tree came croaking down on top of my Porsche.

As you can imagine, I've crashed many, many cars in my time, too many, so I've learned how to lean into it, as they say. Nothing caught fire – a good sign. I crawled out the passenger window. No gas leaks, but the axle holding the right front tire had snapped and was dangling like a badly broken leg. Stuck for the frigid night, I climbed back in and checked my mobile. No signal. I rolled up the window and made myself comfortable, resigned to running the engine all night for warmth and some local radio. Someone would eventually come along. In my case, someone always does. With wet snow falling on the windshield, hot air rushing through the vents, Slovakian rock radio breaking in and out of static at low volume, I fell into a pensive mood.

Let me tell you what's been bothering me, what's been gnawing away at my conscience. The people who work for my father have the gall to underestimate me. I see it in their eyes everywhere I go, I hear it in their measured tones as they contemplate how to say what they're about to say. They might wonder, incredulously, how I could orchestrate my father's kidnapping. How can I be as cunning and calculating as they are? How am I capable of subjecting a frail, elderly man to such a deplorable act as kidnapping? I suppose the most honest answer is because I myself have been under house arrest since the day I was born, by my father, the General and all the people who make up their circle. I've been chained to this bed that is the presidency for five years. This is my chance to escape.

I remember the night that Pa had a stroke in 2006. I was summoned by the General to his bedside for an emergency meeting of his caucus, the first time I'd actually been invited to such a meeting. I looked down on him lying there, tubes running out his nose and his arms, machinery gauging his pulse, his breathing. A cameraman in the room recording the whole thing. I mistakenly believed I was there because he was down to his last moments, that he had regrets, that he wanted to atone for his mistakes. But no.

"How much longer does he have?" I asked.

"It's difficult to say," the General replied. "The doctors think that if he makes it through the next 48 hours, he stands a pretty good chance at recovery."

"Oh," I said, a little disappointed. "Then why am I here?"

"Because we need to consider the question of succession."

"You must have a candidate in mind. One of those guys in the next room," I gestured to the double doors, behind which the members of his inner circle sat smoking and waiting.

"We've all discussed it, and it's been decided that the administration needs a new face, new blood, a younger generation. It needs you."

"What makes you think I'm even interested?" I said. "I've got a Grand Prix race to prepare for in three weeks. There's a big sponsorship deal in the works. Marlboro may finally be coming around to supporting my car. I'm in the prime of my career."

"Think it through, Vadim. Your country is calling you back to your true purpose. You've always been in line for this role, just as Mustafa was. He was once an athlete too. He gave that up for his father's name, to continue this dream."

Seeing him lying there unconscious, seemingly smirking at me from behind that puffed-up face of his, I became quietly furious. "He's spent his life taking all the money the world has to offer, murdered anyone and everyone who voted against him, including our entire extended family, turned my mother insane, corrupted almost every single institution his own father built, and now he gets to sneak off to a noble end."

The old man stirred like a ghost at the rising tenor of my voice.

"Come," said the General, "let's leave him to rest and go talk in the other room."

In the sunken living room whose floor-to-ceiling windows overlooked Revolution Square, we sat down with the inner circle of my pa's feared regime, his ministers of finance, security, and foreign affairs, while his ministers of industry and information played billiards, ashing Cuban cigars on the snow-white bearskin carpet my father had once received as a gift from the prime minister of Canada. A silent maid slipped past periodically to hand-vacuum their droppings, and at the kitchen counter beyond the billiards table, two security guards in leather jackets played cards. I had known these men, who had bags under their eyes and cognac on their breath, all my life, had grown up running between their legs and stealing their cigarettes on the handful of visits home I'd make from boarding school every year and, later, when they were eager to attend my Formula One rallies. Like the General, they had been with my father since the beginning of his presidency, and a few even dated back to my grandfather's administration.

"We've had many talks about this moment," said the ballooning Minister of Finance, a short man who everyone had quietly noted for his inexplicably rapid weight gain that year – meds, it turned out, an entire era of men in twilight. "Your father knew such a day would come, and we planned ahead so there would be no surprises, no panic."

"Even if he recovers," said the Minister of Security, who had only four fingers on his left hand from an incident of torture years back, "his mind is not going to be the same. He knows this. At his age, he wants to retire from being the face of the government."

"He's adamant that you become the new face, Vadim," said the General. "He says you'll grow into it, just as he did."

"Surely one of you is more qualified," I said.

"We all are," said the Minister of Foreign Affairs. "We've built this government and this country. But we're all bureaucrats, too accustomed to working in private to ever have the charisma needed to be the face of the nation. We would be there for you. Nothing would have to change."

"And if he lives?" I said, knowing that my pa, despite his most pragmatic intentions, could never give up controlling the apparatus he'd built.

"Then he lives," said the General. "He'll be on board as an advisor, someone with experience and a network of connections."

"I can't do it. I don't want to do it."

"Vadim, let's be realistic. This is Bleed country," said the Minister of Information through the haze of cigar smoke hanging over the billiards table. "This place has never had a day without a Bleed in charge. As long as there is a Bleed alive, then he will be the face. Think of your grandfather."

"As long as that man is breathing," I gestured to the bedroom, "then I won't get to do a single thing. I'll be a puppet."

"Change takes time," said the General. "Sure, there will be a transition. Let people get to know you. Settle into the driver's seat and take a few laps to see how the car drives. But how much longer do you think he'll live, Vadim? He's an old man. He just suffered a major stroke."

"Find someone else. I'm not going to spend my life protecting his ambitions like a museum guard."

"What do you think will happen once the Americans get wind of the fact that someone new is in charge?" asked the Minister of Finance.

"We'll be done," the General said. "If this administration goes, we'll lose everything. In a heartbeat. Don't you think the vultures have been circling for years, that attempts haven't been made? You're a young man. You have a lifetime to make this country in your image."

"It's the 21st century," I moaned. "The world out there is different. Everyone wants elections."

"Your father has won every election put before him. So will you."

"Forget it."

The old men went quiet, recognizing we'd arrived at an impasse. The General said, "Vadim, we'd much rather have you want this. It's easier for everyone."

"You included," the Minister of Foreign Affairs chimed in.

"What does that mean?"

"It's just that your father, he has control over all your finances. Even the money in your own accounts. There are reams of paperwork involved, he has many lawyers and bank managers working on this, but the upshot is that he set it up that way to compel you down the same path as him. He thought, *he thinks*, I should say, that you'll come around as you grow older and begin to see the world differently."

What would you have done? I wasn't willing to give up the deluxe lifestyle that I'd always known, and this leash of legacy, I already knew, had a way of yanking back on my neck no matter how many times I tried to pull it off. I suppose I'd always known that this moment, or some variation of it, would come.

THE NATION

MAHBAD'S NEWS SOURCE SINCE 1964

23 Dead, Dozens More Injured

Bleed calls for pro-government rally at Revolution Square

BY NADA FERBER

Violence flared across Qala Phratteh last night and 23 people were confirmed killed as opposition supporters aligned with Fatma Gavras defied the government's curfew and took to the streets to again demand the release of election results.

Doctors at nearby hospitals said they are overwhelmed by burn, shooting and shrapnel victims.

In the city's west-end Lezer districts, anti-government protesters burned tires and overturned cars, blocking off major arteries. Snipers lined rooftops, converting the neighbourhood's narrow streets into shooting galleries for the police forces that tried to dismantle the barricades. Police had to retreat and call in military units.

The military response to the snipers was forceful. For the first time since 1983, tanks fired into a city neighbourhood. Witnesses said the shelling of residential apartments was indiscriminate. Residents reported no advance warning before the operation, which knocked down parts of buildings and set fire to many more.

Caught between the government and opposition forces, residents hurried out into the night in pyjamas and housecoats, clutching crying children to their chests. Medical personnel accused the military of keeping emergency aid away from the burning buildings, even as the critically injured emerged.

According to General Constantin Benini, the opposition firepower is evidence that the New Nationalists Party is being overtaken by more extreme elements that may be behind the kidnapping of Mustafa Bleed. The government is not commenting on its investigations into the elder Bleed's whereabouts.

Still abroad, President Vadim Bleed has put out a call for restraint on all sides, and for the release of his father. Despite growing sectarian tensions, the government has called for a demonstration of Bleed supporters – what it deems "the silent majority."

Tomorrow night's pro-government rally is intended to project that Vadim Bleed is the legitimate winner of the election. But it also sets up a dangerous clash at Revolution Square, where opposition supporters have been demonstrating nightly since election results were first postponed.

Mustafa Bleed

CAN YOU HEAR THE EMERGENCY sirens? I had those installed in the city's infrastructure during my mid-90s mission to modernize the valley's power grid into one of the world's leading surveillance mechanisms. That must mean an operation is underway. I've never heard the full breadth of my ambitious system set into motion before. Even though I only managed a few hours' sleep, it's cheering me up a little. The largest shopping complex in the country will not open for business today. Though I can't see them from here, if my review of "state of emergency" protocol holds accurate, right about now tanks should be rolling down Blanco Bleed Boulevard to cordon off the government brain trust.

I'm standing on the long balcony, waiting for the fog to dissipate in the fresh mountain air. The sun came up over the Allegory Mountains about an hour ago, and I can see only patches of the city through the overgrown trees. Smoke from a fire is billowing over the valley. How I wish I had binoculars. All the minor details are what ultimately tell a story. I'm trying to make out what's burning, because it looks like the fire might be near Revolution Square.

If not for these overgrown trees, I'd see all of Qala Phratteh from up here. This is why the British chose this location in the first place, to have a living map of the capital. I had this trivia erased from all our school history textbooks a long time ago now, so the only people who would still remember those times are my age. As a little boy back in the '30s, I used to come here with my father. Way back when he was a Boran tribal leader, my father was paid to correspond back and forth between the British and the Boran people. Many people don't remember that anymore. Back in pre-independence times, we Borans had nothing.

There was a knock at the door. A cadet walked in. "British ambassador Louise Pressinger here to see you, sir."

"Then don't keep her waiting."

I had nothing to offer her in terms of hospitality. No semi-facing armchairs in front of the fireplace, no assortment of breakfast teas, not even a discreet secretary to whom I could dictate orders. I was still in the same clothes I arrived in, and I probably smelled. No doubt she'll disapprove of what they've done to me here. I've yet to see Louise approve of anything in 27 years of relations.

"Come in, Louise," I said, clasping her hand. "Sit on this piano bench, please. How did you know to find me here?"

"I've been in touch with General Benini."

"Who else knows about his plans?"

"No one. I'm not even convinced he knows what he intends to do. He's a very impenetrable person. He only allowed me access to you because you're technically on British soil at the moment, and he needs my cooperation."

"Tell me, Louise, have you heard from Vadim?"

"We've got our people watching him."

"Where?"

"Out of the way. Slovakia maybe."

"Why on earth Slovakia?"

"Why not?" She knew the history. With Vadim, there's no controlling where he ends up. All we can do is follow along and wait for the right moment to intervene.

"Why are you not supporting him more? This election should be his to take. Our family has worked hard for your interests for half a century."

"We have a new Minister of Foreign Affairs. He's young. He's from the other party."

"This is the problem with democracy. No one remembers any of the commitments they make. It's all theatrical bluster and nothing ever gets done."

"Oh, we remember, Mustafa. It's the New Nationalists we can't control. Fatma Gavras has been courting the Americans, who are convinced that it's time for regime change."

"The Americans? But the Americans are supposed to be on our side."

"They say they want meaningful change through elections."

"What does that mean? We just had an election. We have the results, and the deck has already been reshuffled. According to the same plan that has always been in place."

Louise sighed. "Why didn't Vadim do more to keep everyone happy? It wouldn't have been so hard."

"Ah." I knew then what this was all about. "This comes down to land leases."

"Among other things."

"Tell me, is the General with the Americans too?"

"Right now, the General is a problem for everyone. This is why I've gerrymandered this time with you. This bloody crackdown he's orchestrating is a complication for us all. It's off script. We all need to be a lot calmer right now."

"And the General agreed to giving away my location like this? Even though he's a thorn in your side."

"He's calculating, like everyone else. He needs to keep one channel open with us. As long as Vadim's in Europe, we effectively have your president."

"Is that a threat?"

"Talk to the General."

"You wouldn't dare."

"Why don't you let the election results tell the truth and move on with your life, Mustafa?"

"I wouldn't know what to do with myself."

"Think about it. Glad to see you're okay. I'll be in touch."

And with that, she picked up her attaché case and left. I walked out to the balcony, and from there I could hear her diplomatic security detail driving off down the winding gravel road.

Vadim Bleed

WHEN I WOKE UP A few hours later, it was still dark and my bones had become brittle from the impact and the cold. I couldn't sit there much longer. Towards morning, a pair of headlights cut through the darkness and, soon after, a rickety produce truck piled high with onions came rattling down the road. I flashed my headlights with the little battery power left, climbed out the frosted window and flagged down the driver, who was gracious enough to offer me a ride to the next town. He was the sturdy backwoods type, white hair, calloused hands, missing teeth, and I couldn't understand a word he spoke beyond his generous wave to jump aboard. So we sat quietly as the truck navigated its way along the potholed and winding highway, a baby billy goat braying for cashews at my knee. The driver tried to explain with various hand motions why the animal had to sit up front. I understood that he would eat too many onions if he were left in the back.

I was tired, physically and mentally drained. The night in the cold had left me feeling uncharacteristically dour, and not just because I crashed a brand-new Porsche. Porsches, I like to say, can be replaced. Bad memories can't. They can only be stowed away in the mind's garage, under tarp, and left behind a closed door. But they don't disappear. Their value grows volatile. And there's never been a closed door that hasn't opened again.

The onion truck dropped me off at a farmers' market in the city of Trenčín. I staggered through the medieval town, my exhausted, over-reflective thoughts distorted by the imposing gothic architecture, the eerily calm surface of the Váh River.

"Hotel?" I mouthed, slowly and loudly, to a hunched-over gypsy as she pushed a vegetable cart toward the market. I flashed five stars with my hands. She murmured something incomprehensible and tried to raise her right arm, which proved difficult. Not wanting to appear rude, I gave her a red onion in thanks, which I'd stowed away in my pocket, and then continued on my way. A moment later, I saw the onion roll past my feet.

Rain clouds hung heavy over the market square. Thunder rumbled off in the distance, ready to ignite a downpour. Hurriedly jogging past a three-star hotel, I turned away from the river and roamed the hilly streets in search of a suitable place to lay my head. At last I found a Marriott and, feeling the first large drops of rain on my forehead, I decided to sacrifice a star from my standards and stepped inside.

"Your best room," I said absentmindedly, pulling off my racing gloves.

"Of course, sir," replied the concierge.

I slapped a platinum card on the marble counter and tossed my valise to the nearest bellboy. "What floor?"

"Room 400," the concierge said, handing me the key. "Shall we bill all incidentals to your room?"

"As you wish."

I walked confidently toward the elevators, snapping my fingers at the bellboy to carry my bag. Upstairs, I tipped him generously. "Go have fun."

I undressed and sat down on the bidet, closed my eyes, and breathed deeply as warm water jetted briskly into my backside. Then I poured a hot bath and soaked in the steamy tub until my fingers had wrinkled. My ribs were still sore from the accident. I would write a letter to Porsche once I got home, I decided, decrying their forceful airbags. Finally I was clean and ready for bed, which was enough for now. I realized I was alone here, unknown, nothing more than a stranger to the peasants in this region. I was free to be whoever I wanted to be. That felt good. I fell asleep picturing a younger version of myself sitting alone in the corner of a café, in an undiscovered city much like this one, charting my thoughts in a little notebook by amber candlelight, as the world bustled along around me.

When I woke up, it was dark. A night breeze, in collaboration with windows left open all day, had conspired to chill the room and give me a stiff neck. I sat up wearily, contemplated staying in bed till morning, whenever that was, and decided that, no, I was too hungry for that. Forgetting for a moment that I wasn't in my own bed, I reached for the bell I normally keep on my nightstand. Of course it wasn't there, and for a moment I felt homesick, as if I'd been travelling for too long. It had been days now since I'd checked in with my administration. How had that election sorted itself out? For the first time I wondered if my pa was in any real danger. The distance had softened my instincts. Oh well. The beauty of managing chaos was that you could step back and ignore it, let others exhaust themselves trying to get a handle on what was going on. I checked the time: only nine o'clock. The accident had shaken me more than I'd first thought. I needed to clear my head and come to terms with what had happened.

After taking the elevator down to the lobby, I walked through the hotel's revolving doors, out onto the quiet street. When I'd abandoned my staff in Vienna, I'd needed my own space to formulate a plan, to think earnestly about the future. But now I just felt out of orbit. I began to doubt whether it had been a good idea to be so compliant about my pa's kidnapping. Sure, it wasn't so horrible if the Russians had done me a favour in the long run, but increasingly I was beginning to see how it might be perceived as a sign of weakness to have others come in and carve up the Bleeds to their liking. I should've taken charge of the ambitious idea from the beginning, had my men do it themselves. Now I was in someone else's debt.

I found a mysterious neon-lit door in a nearby alley that led down to a basement nightclub done entirely in bathroom tile and smoked glass. Slouching along the bar, I thought back to my first days in office. I'd presented blueprints and maps, had slideshows made outlining all the socio-political benefits I'd internalized at university, and not one parliamentarian on either side of the aisle wanted to hear it. They were all stuck in my father's world order.

By the last sips of my fourth drink, the sleepy bar had emptied out, and the only two other people left in the place were employees cleaning up. I resolved to walk the night and air out my lungs, maybe find an after-party or corral the local castle's inhabitants to join me for a nightcap at my hotel if it wasn't too embarrassing for them to spend time at a Marriott. I'd slept all day and so I wasn't exactly tired. Making my way up the basement stairs, I stumbled out the metal door and into the alley, where the doorman locked up behind me and turned off the small neon sign, leaving me in complete darkness. I began walking nowhere in particular. I walked along the empty streets, looking into dark shop windows and generally wondering if I would find an open restaurant to serve me the long-delayed meal that had sent me out into the night in the first place. I walked several blocks and found nothing. It was nearing midnight on what I assumed was a weeknight – I honestly couldn't tell you what day it was – and this town was fast asleep.

I decided, finally, to find my way back to the hotel and order room service and perhaps another bottle of champagne to while away the night in front of the television. The hotel couldn't have been that far off, as I was pretty sure I'd only walked around the corner to arrive at the bar, but as I tried to retrace my steps I discovered to my dismay that all the streets looked the same. As I searched for a familiar landmark, I began to sense that I wasn't alone after all. The streets were still eerily silent, but now and again I heard a car behind me. I turned a corner to see if they would fade away, but there it was again, lingering.

Worried, I broke into a light jog, searching for a well-lit plaza or a policeman to guide me back to my hotel. The engine grew louder. I looked over my shoulder, only to be blinded by headlights. Someone drove up beside me and beckoned me with an open car door.

My Visit from the Secret Police & Other Stories of Freedom Derailed

by Kaarina Faasol

I'm comforted by the fact that so many of you read my last blog. The letters many of you have written in support were both unexpected and necessary, to keep me writing even as the very people I criticize have begun to tighten their vices. I usually don't offer up the details of my personal circumstances too openly. Beyond questions of journalistic professionalism, our nation isn't the safest place for a writer these days. But today I'll break from convention to share the news that my apartment was vandalized last night.

This wasn't your typical robbery. The whole place was turned upside down, but nothing was taken. My laptop was open on my kitchen table, not where I'd left it. My blog post was open on the screen. There was a strange USB key in it containing all my files, as if someone wanted to say, "Look, we can come in and take anything we want to, whenever we like." I was only gone out to dinner. Someone knew I was away and how to pull this off quickly while I was gone.

This is not the first time I've been harassed by police. But something about this feels more organized and dangerous. This state of personal siege appears to have quickly become the new normal for many people, ever since the Ministry of the Interior declared that it would leave no stone unturned in its search for Mustafa Bleed. In the past few days, the Bleed government has sought to turn the tables on this election. Every person in this crumbling nation is now considered a stone.

It seems I've gotten off lightly, compared to some others. Since my last post, the fiancé of Fatma Gavras's cousin was pulled away from a family dinner and hasn't been seen again. "The message is for me," she's told me. "Everyone knew it. My cousin called me first. They won't even bother notifying the police."

My publishing colleagues at *The Nation* say the Ministry of the Interior is now openly wrestling with the editors for control over all lead articles. Editor Nada Ferber tells me she's begun receiving messages from the Ministry of Foreign Affairs, who would like her to come in to answer questions about her passport. "I'm afraid they'll confiscate it. Or worse, me."

Still others have suffered worse fates. Contained in the news that Ferber is barred from reporting, three more New Nationalists Party candidates disappeared overnight. One of them, an acquaintance I'd only met twice before in social circles, turned up dead this morning in the middle of a busy intersection. Sectarian kidnappings have gripped the country in the past two days. There's a real fear we're about to slip back into dark times, a disturbing echo of the events that led to the civil war of the '80s.

Meanwhile, practically anyone who cast a ballot for the NNP has a story of a car being impounded or is facing exorbitant fines for invented offences. "They want us to shut up by raising the consequences," says Gavras. "They know we have more to lose than they do. But I'm ready to lose everything." Gavras is already losing a lot. Her last rally at Revolution Square sparked a wave of violence across Qala Phratteh that resulted in 137 dead – the official figure in the papers was only 23. That's not deterring her from preparing for another rally at Revolution Square, where protesters have met every night since the election. "It's too late to stop now. We'll come back every night, until they make every last one of us disappear."

Back at New Nationalists headquarters, the atmosphere has clouded over with resignation. Dabny Bolshoi has effectively conceded the election. "Gavras's plan requires so many people to die for what they believe in," he says. "She's raising the stakes to the point where no one can control the outcome anymore. That's not politics. It's war. I was there before when this happened the first time with Independence United. We lost so much more than we gained."

Vadim Bleed

"DON'T WORRY, MR. BLEED, I'm not interested in harming you," said an elderly Chinese man smoking a cigarette in the shadowy backseat. "I am only a concerned customer trying to benefit us both."

I climbed in the back. "You had my father kidnapped," I ventured. The car began to move again.

"Whatever was decided, that's between you and others. The power dynamic between father and son, between son and state, between state and supporters, is not ideal for our future business, wouldn't you agree?

"How did you find me?"

"Mr. Bleed, let me get to the point. The Americans have lost faith in you. Time is short, the consequences unpleasant. The longer the question of your leadership hangs in the air, the further we move away from new partnerships."

"The Americans don't want to negotiate. They only want to dictate terms."

"We are not interested in buying uranium from the Americans, Mr. Bleed. They have endless regulations, control tactics, and cost inflations at every turn. We are interested in buying uranium directly from you, a better deal for everyone."

"I would love nothing more than to be rid of the whole mining conglomerate. Can you do that?"

"Infrastructure can be bought and sold, but only in times of greater certainty. Mr. Bleed, I cannot stress to you enough how important it is that you go back home as soon as possible."

"I'm sure General Benini is working on the matter as we speak."

"Leadership, Mr. Bleed. The public image of leadership has more currency than any backroom deal. A door has been opened for you, but you have yet to take advantage. Others look at this story and see only an open door, not you. You must examine the advice you've been given. You must question every speaker's intentions."

"Even yours."

"Even mine, Mr. Bleed. Nothing is set in stone, except for the minerals we need. Everything else must adapt in a changing world."

"Who are you?"

"I am someone who's not here, Mr. Bleed. I am your conscience, a finger pointing you out of the forest and back to the path. We have ambitions in robotics, telecommunications that will propel your country forward many years, if only you take advantage. In the end, your father and grandfather's achievements, they will pale in comparison to what you can accomplish, if only you don't let this opportunity go to waste."

The car pulled up in front of my hotel, and the driver climbed out to open my door.

THE NATION

MAHBAD'S NEWS SOURCE SINCE 1964

Bleeds Must Go

Editorial board endorses public outcry for new government

BY NADA FERBER

Despite the consequences to our livelihoods, the editorial board of *The Nation* has decided to endorse the growing calls for Vadim Bleed to step down.

Well before the election, Mr. Bleed had lost his credibility to govern. Unemployment has spiked over the past five years, as has the cost of most basic goods. Efforts to diversify the economy, a central promise of his first campaign, have either stagnated or never materialized.

Since the election, a troubling cycle of violence has taken hold that threatens to erase the three decades of relative calm since the civil war of the 1980s. Meanwhile, relations between the government and the foreign-owned mining industry have deteriorated to an all-time low as the administration jockeys for a greater share of mining royalties.

In order to hold onto power, Bleed appears to have resorted to the same deadly manoeuvres that led his father Mustafa Bleed into civil war in 1983. Both then and now, a legacy candidate who lost the popular vote refuses to recognize the people's will. Using the full might of the state security apparatus, he divides and conquers through a series of bloody events that embolden sectarian animosities between the Boran majority and the Lezer underclass.

Vadim Bleed's tactics are carbon copies of his father's handiwork. The kidnapping of Mustafa Bleed has scrambled efforts to release election ballots, a convenience in timing that cannot be ignored. In the kidnappings, murders, and outright massacres that have come since, the ideals of democracy recede further from the spotlight until, as a society, we find ourselves lost in another fog of war.

We cannot let that happen again. Last time, 26,000 Lezers died over four years, and untold others fled the country, never to return. We are still paying the price for those losses. Our society is on another precipice now. We cannot underestimate the cautions that our own history offers at this moment. The opportunity still exists to avoid falling into another abyss. We cannot stand silent as more atrocities unfold in the name of protecting the Bleeds.

We do not arrive at such a decision lightly. We are fully aware of this newspaper's origins and history in relation to the Bleeds. With this call, we risk our own employment and the very foundations of this newspaper.

Mustafa Bleed

I MUST ADMIT, HERE, that I'm beginning to tear up a little. My bed sheets are damp where I've pressed my face and grieved in private. This has been an emotionally trying time. I've never gone this long without my pills, and the world is beginning to tilt off-kilter. Entire sections of the room are sliding around.

When I can, I stand on the balcony and witness what this city must endure to become mine again. I can't help but wonder if it's worth it. It's late afternoon in the capital, and I've been hearing the static stutter of gunfire and the thud of explosions down below all day. I desperately try to make out what is going on through the foliage, but I only succeed in hurting my eyes.

The valley has been flushed of all the usual noises that make Qala Phratteh a home. A normal day in the capital would bring a cacophony of car horns competing with the din of buskers. Now only emergency sirens blare, warning people to stay off the streets or risk arrest. Two plumes of smoke rise up to cloud the city skies, one from the factory district and a second from Revolution Square.

Events must not be unfolding as planned. I know because I've just had a visit from the General to assure me that they are. Contrary to previous visits, he was dressed in camouflage combat fatigues instead of the usual medal-studded uniform.

"I'm so sorry for this," he gestured at the room around us.

"I have no staff, no clothes. Where is my doctor?"

"Nothing gets done unless I do it myself. I'll take care of this, don't worry."

"Come, walk with me." In part for my own balance, I led him by the hand to the open balcony. "It's quite the view that the British had from here. You can see a car driving along the other side of the Allegory Mountains on a clear day. If this overgrowth wasn't here, I would be able to see everything from this balcony. Now, I can only hear the artillery and see the smoke."

"It's unfortunate how the opposition is reacting. They have their people out in the thousands. They're more organized than we anticipated. Ordinary people keep joining them wherever they march."

"They're getting bold. This is what I feared would happen once Vadim stopped throwing them in jail. What is it that they want? It can't just be a question of Vadim."

"They want a revolution. We've shot at them, clubbed them from horseback, fired all kinds of gases. They want a complete reinvention of government."

"My father already did that. I spent decades making sure the government stayed reinvented."

"I know. I was there at your side."

"It's the new generation," I complained. "They have no long-term memory. Everyone who was there with us is old or dead. We over-educate them and then appease their laziness."

"They complain there are no jobs and that food is expensive."

"People used to farm. Now they just want the work and its spoils handed to them." I sighed and changed the subject. "I had a visit from Louise."

"Yes, I know. She insisted, threatened to pull SUMCAX out of negotiations once and for all. Be careful what you say to her. She has many people's interests in mind, and yours are not among them."

"Vadim is somewhere in Europe."

"If he sets foot here, there will be a price on his head. We're keeping him away until we can control the situation on the ground."

"Yes, keep him away," I reluctantly agreed. "He never wanted any of this on his shoulders. He's not equipped to handle it now."

"We wanted to save him the embarrassment of returning to certain defeat."

"But it looks like exile now," I complained, unable to hold back my frustrations any longer. "Like he couldn't care less. My son is being kept out of the country, and I'm locked up here. For the first time in our country's history, there isn't a Bleed in charge. No wonder they want a second, unnecessary revolution out there. They smell weakness."

"The military is in charge for the time being, sir," he said, doing his best to placate me.

"Then send a clear message. Crush this irritating uprising and let's get on with the plan," I demanded. "Stop pussyfooting. Find a way to arrest Bolshoi, arrest that doctor who talks too much for her own good, execute them in public, and then announce my interim return to the presidency. Will through

134

force, Constantin. Force is the only discipline that can break their momentum."

"That's what we'll do, sir." The General clicked his heels together and offered an enthusiastic salute.

"And for the love of god, find my pills. I'm an octogenarian."

He kissed my hand, and then walked backward out the ballroom doors, and I lay down for a rest that turned into a long nap. I don't recall falling asleep, but it was already getting dark by the time I was stirred awake again by the sound of gunfire. It was no longer echoing up randomly from the valley below, but concentrated in streaks of light and explosions from Revolution Square.

Clashing Demonstrations End in Bloodbath

by Kaarina Faasol

I come to you tonight having survived an orchestrated massacre at Revolution Square. I write this entry immensely dejected, driven forward only by the fact that so many of you appear to be reading these words. For that I am eternally grateful. I never once thought that this sidestep in my writing career, an afterthought from a disillusioned career journalist, would turn into my life's mission. I want you to feel my despair because I have no way of hiding it at the moment. I wish it weren't so.

In the past hours, I have seen literally hundreds killed or injured, and untold numbers arrested who will most likely never be heard from again. There are tanks still roving Revolution Square, indiscriminately crushing dead bodies. Soldiers are shooting anyone who steps into the square to help those who are dying. Hospitals are overwhelmed with casualties and scores more dead still lie unattended in the streets surrounding the large plaza. The echo of gunfire can be heard everywhere across the city.

The twin demonstrations planned for tonight were designed to collide from the start. The opposition forces led by Fatma Gavras had been occupying the square nightly ever since Vadim Bleed refused to release the election results. Shortly after dusk, a sea of pro-government supporters marched to Revolution Square via three boulevards to the east, speakers atop army-issued jeeps inciting the crowd. At that point, the lights surrounding the square went out. The bright trails of Molotov cocktails began to fly from the pro-government side, into the dark occupied by sequestered opposition protesters. When they tried to break through the barricade, the police opened fire.

Trapped in complete darkness between police on one side and pro-Bleed demonstrators on the other, the screams of the opposition protesters began to fill the night. Those farther back, like myself, who were fortunate enough to escape past the police lines, discovered that the rooftops of the surrounding streets were lined with snipers equipped with night-vision goggles, taking aim at anyone who crossed their purview.

After circumventing censors and publishing a damning denunciation of the Bleed government, editors at *The Nation* tell me they have been barred from their offices. "Everything you read now is being written by the Ministry of the Interior," says editor Nada Ferber. "They've taken my passport and have all of us under watch. I don't know how much longer I'll be here."

Was this massacre the beginning of another genocide? An overwhelming majority of dead and injured were Lezers. My clothes are still soaked in their blood. I tried to save them, and I failed. My lungs are still burning with chemicals and the smoke of so many fires. We cannot stand by and silently watch another genocide unfold just 30 years after Mustafa Bleed and General Benini got away with orchestrating the murder of 26,000 Lezers.

All I can do in the face of these images that will surely haunt me till the end of my days is write them down, document them in the hope that someone on the outside will learn what happened. I have no way of giving you hard numbers, and frankly I worry more and more for my own life every day, but I feel deeply that I must continue no matter what happens.

Mustafa Bleed

THE GUNFIRE HAS FINALLY STOPPED, for now. The darkness has tempered and dawn should soon break through, so that may be why. Oh, how my head throbs. Just yesterday I found the humidity of this room stifling, but today I can't shiver the coldness out of my bones. I've had a long life, a very long life. I've made decisions, too many to suit the moment, always aware that somewhere there must be consequences that weren't considered, that my decisiveness would one day come back to bite me. Now it feels like I have an entire lifetime of decisions behind me, nipping at my heels.

I'm remembering, in a feverish infinite loop, a few days of my life in particular, after the civil war. Much like Vadim, the General and I once broke free from our responsibilities too. Being who we are can be overwhelming at times. We drove the northern coast of the Mediterranean all the way to Cannes to attend the film festival. It was the first year our country had an entry make the competition, and the film in question had ended up there on the coattails of our national turmoil, as a statement of support from the rest of the world. The film was called *A People Rising*. At three hours and 46 minutes, the agitprop epic was also the longest film chosen for the competition that year.

We decided on the trip one evening after the official selections were announced, after we'd shared more than a few cognacs during one of my post-talk show soirées. Putting down the Lezer uprising had been a tense and physically taxing experience. We'd spent the better part of those early years of my presidency on high alert. Films were one of the few entertainments we both enjoyed. And besides, we had professional interests in the back of our minds with *A People Rising*. The film had been directed and produced by Milos Estami, a vocal supporter of the '83 uprising whose whereabouts were unknown. He was expected to attend the screening. We supposed that if he didn't win the Palme d'Or or at least the Grand Prize, we'd have a worthy excuse to have him followed and arrested.

Few jurors were capable of lasting through a poetic silent film in which a three-legged German shepherd hobbles through the Allegory Mountains from one village to the next, in search of good deeds to perform. Introducing the film, Estami explained that it was intended to be a treatise on how our country had lost its moral compass. He appeared so confident during his pre-screening interview in front of a sympathetic audience, unaware we were there in the dark, watching him.

It was almost midnight when the film finally let out and the few attendees who'd made it to the very end staggered away rubbing their eyes. Still delirious from the hallucinogenic aurora borealis that marked the film's protracted finale, the General and I set out on foot through the narrow streets of Cannes in search of a bistro where we could finally sit down to dinner. Back home, the war's fallout had subsided and many of the key opposition figures had either been jailed, harassed into exile, or quietly assassinated, and here we were in a foreign country, out in public without our official uniforms for the first time since the election campaign, and in that moment we realized without saying a word that we were able to walk the streets that night without looking over our shoulders. We were briefly anonymous, two filmgoers wandering the night after their movie, left awkwardly free to stroll the cobblestone streets under the golden glow of lampposts, discussing the merits of the yachts along the piers and generally exchanging comments about the strangers we passed.

We found a little place where the kitchen was still open, a corner restaurant with a vacant table for two on its awning-covered terrace and, there, surrounded by the chatter of millionaires and movie industry people, we sat down and began insulting the picture we'd just endured. Soon the boeuf bourguignon, escargot, and braised elk we'd ordered arrived, followed by wine from the restaurant's private stock.

"To your father's legacy," I remember the General toasting.

"To our military," I added, "and to you, for helping us steer the country in the right direction."

Our glasses clinked.

We finished that bottle and another before the end of our meal, and with the terrace emptying out by three in the morning, we convinced the waiter into selling us a bottle of cognac for the walk back to the hotel. I was somehow wearing a sailor's cap by then, most likely a gift from one of the diners at the next table, with whom we'd laughed a lot at some point along the way, and as we swayed through the side streets in search of a taxi, we passed the cognac back and forth between us and balanced on each other's shoulders when we had to relieve ourselves in dark alleys, and it felt for the first time as if we were not president and military general, but simply friends.

We got a little carried away that night, and the empty bottle of cognac ended up shattering the display window of an Yves Saint Laurent storefront. At the sound of the alarm, we cracked up like schoolboys and ran all the way to our hotel, as if our diplomatic immunity meant nothing.

Back at the hotel we crawled to the end of the hall where our suite was located. There, we stripped down to our briefs and settled into the sauna, where we slurred through our deeply held philosophies on life and friendship. Exhausted, as the sun rose, we retired to our respective chambers. To this day, I can't think of a single memory from my political life that has kept me as warm as that one.

The next day, there was so much to do. We had Milos Estami quietly arrested at the Cannes airport. He was hooded and gagged, and put on a military flight back home. For the damage to his flagship storefront, Yves Saint Laurent personally called our hotel suite that morning to berate us with xenophobic platitudes. Western Europeans have historically remained cold to us. With the baffling hangovers that had set in, we began the long trip back home, more sombre than expected.

Yet even after everyone had duly been paid off and the fallout of our film-festival escapade had settled, the air between the General and me was unrecognizable from the night before. We were, after all, headed back to our official posts, I thought, no longer free to run the streets in casual wear as Mustafa and Constantin, but relegated once again to our hardened post-war images of fearsome president and rampant military general.

Ten days after our return to Qala Phratteh, I decided to have the arrested Milos Estami on my nightly program for a gru-

elling interview that would very publicly delve into his political views, and perhaps even garner a confession or recantation.
I arranged for the episode to be followed with a grossly cen-
sored version of *A People Rising* itself, for anyone who wanted
to stay up all night and risk suicide by boredom. I thought it
would be an opportunity to assert my views on our culture, a
chance to list our great forefathers while dropping subtle hints
about the direction I'd like to see our collective creativity take,
so we wouldn't end up with more international embarrass-
ments to stain our reputation.

In an attempt to rekindle our Cannes connection, I invited
the General to join us for the interview, to make the appearance less of a one-on-one and more of a spontaneous conversation. I genuinely thought the talk would provide some
worthy insights into the nature of film, but the warm and
good-humoured cinephile I knew to be hidden within Constantin didn't emerge that evening, and all I got instead was a
sternly uniformed official drone who used his time on air to
threaten the director, warn the country not to follow in his
footsteps, and speak patriotically of his military's ability to
put down the uprising. I tried to lighten the mood, to no avail.
Needless to say, Estami was devastated with fear, could not
unleash a true clash of ideologies, and what began simply as
a studio session wafting with the stench of fear soon segued
into another one of my ad-libbed monologues when the director fainted at the distress caused by the General's interro-
gation techniques.

By the end of it, I had to cut him off, if I remember correctly, with a sharp slap of my hand against my desk. The
sound shot across the airwaves, reminding him who was in
charge in front of the whole country. It was bad television. I

don't care for on-air surprises like that. Even though I do possess the unusual gift of being able to salvage any situation, I'd sooner be in control than let events spontaneously devolve like that.

Afterward, I pulled the General aside in the green room and asked, "What do you think you're doing? This isn't some basement torture chamber. We have a national audience. Maybe you don't understand the subtleties of the medium."

He couldn't even look me in the eye.

"Well, what do you have to say for yourself?" I pressed him against the wall to force an answer. "Speak up, man."

"I can't humour a state prisoner for entertainment," the General confessed. "It goes against everything I believe in."

"The man with many faces always trumps his opponent. What you just did in there, everyone knows exactly who you are. You're the suppressor of an uprising, someone who doesn't know how or when to move on and build on his victories."

"I am who I am," he replied, and then he saluted me with more than a little contempt and marched off to his dressing room to wash away his television makeup.

I am who I am. This from the man who's now being creative. I thought about what he could mean by that in the days that followed. Who is he, really? I wanted to write him a letter, either an official reprimand or a more intimate confession of how I felt after our night in Cannes, but in the end I held back. The responsibilities of the presidency began to distract me once again. But this morning, 27 years later, as I lie here in pain on this lumpy bed, I'm thinking about that contemptuous salute and those words again for some reason. Didn't he just salute me that way again? They're chasing each other in circles. I am who I am. They won't go away.

Vadim Bleed

Have you ever wondered, like I have, why the weakest piece on a chessboard is the king? What does he do, buried in the back, limited in movement, other than not get taken? Sometimes, when I'm hiding behind all the armoured cars, the missile-launching private jets, all the steroid-infused guards, all the history and all the precedent, I tend to forget I'm even there. I have so many handlers hiving away in my father's machinery, constantly begging me to just let them get on with their work, that I'd like to think the whole apparatus can hum along without its figurehead smiling down on it from up high. I'm better off as a presence that doesn't get in the way, a feeling that's always acknowledged but never felt, a god, a ghost.

PART 3

CONSEQUENCES

Mustafa Bleed

IT'S SO DARK OUT NOW. Tonight, with the electricity cut citywide, the night sky is lit up like a million pinholes in a way I haven't seen since I was a little boy. I've endured almost a week in this musty room, the longest week of my life. I feel delirious, not quite myself. I have no appetite. Any food would help now that I'm feeling this way, agitated in my skin. Were I not here now, were I feeling myself, the normal pace of my days dictates that I would go out driving in one of my collectible race cars, equipped to seat only one, a solitary investment. With the day's traffic evaporated, I can accelerate to speeds upwards of 150 km per hour, blissfully neglecting all traffic lights as the indistinct streaks of bright light and sound melt down to ephemeral blurs.

Maybe you understand, driving this way connects me to my son. This is where Vadim first discovered his obsession with speeding cars; it's one of the rare talents we have in common. Back when he was a motherless toddler, the only time I had for family life would come late, at this hour. Overriding the warnings of his male nannies, I would gently wake him from his sleep, pacify his startled cries with a round of tickles on the floor, and then carry him to the garage, where I would let him choose a car. From there, I would stuff him into what little breathing room existed between my heaving chest and the removable steering wheel, and we'd go flying off into the night. By the time we'd toured the outskirts of Qala Phratteh, where we threaded our path through the herds of wild gazelles that crossed the rural roads at night, and our gas needle was shivering dangerously close to empty, I'd deftly swerve the nimble race car backward into the garage only to find that little Vadim had fallen asleep against my chest somewhere along the way.

Family is a problem that can't be solved, I surmised for the millionth time as I paced back and forth across the balcony in the humid night air. It's my fault. I bought Vadim too many race cars. I allowed too many exemptions from Qala Phratteh's road rules to accommodate his eight-year-old's desire to drive through the city streets just like his pa. A child's desires can seem so precious, so pure at the time.

He was born to a troubled mother, a woman rattled by unpredictable outbursts of rage. We married when I was already in my 40s, if only because my father thought I needed a family man's image. She was much younger, not even 20 years old at the time we were introduced. The marriage lived up to neither of our expectations. When she fled back home, I was left a single parent. I couldn't have made it through those difficult years without an army of shadow parents to care for Vadim while I tended to crisis after impending crisis.

From the age of four, the year my father was murdered, Vadim was afforded the best boarding schools: Switzerland, Norway, Saudi Arabia, Japan. He attended and was eventually expelled from all of them. Headmaster after headmaster reported that he was listless, insolent, given to daydreaming and unresponsive to consequence. He refused to sit for therapy, so I had a stealth team of psychologists assembled to spy on him. They reported that he was making up for the absence of his mother. A mother's love can be so valuable to a boy, its absence so volatile and detrimental, even if when he grows up he realizes that a father's approval is all he's ever needed.

Can I offer some advice to all the fathers out there? Never give a teenager a fully staffed private jet for his birthday. After the initial euphoria of hugs and high-fives subsides and you discover that the cysts of conflict are still roiling in your offspring's heart, he'll take your peace offering and use it to hurt you. When Vadim was 17, he used the gift in question to fly himself to Bulgaria to surprise his estranged mother at her convent. He didn't make it through the weekend. The boy was a stranger to her. She was deeply deranged by then, and he was a reminder of a painful family obligation. Her piousness grew extreme in later years. He flew back, rope scars on his wrists and ankles, jaded and depressed. It was plainly my fault for giving him such an extravagant toy. Soon after, I quietly had the plane hijacked.

I smell trouble in the air. It's pitch black outside still, and fighting has erupted somewhere around the compound, closer than ever before. It sounds like it's right around the corner, at the doors of the Retreat. Someone's trying to break in. Listen. Can you hear men shouting, the roar of jeeps and heavy artillery? I've been taking a look over my balcony all night, to see if I'm being watched and how far down I would fall if I had to jump. I can't sleep. My blood is restless even though I'm, oh, so tired. Shadows lurk everywhere. Perhaps even my imagination is under surveillance.

As I lean over the railing again, to contemplate how the black branches of an evergreen would cushion a crash landing, I hear the double doors of my gallery blow open. In walk two guards I've never seen before, whose faces escape me no matter how hard I try to connect with their eyes. They march out to the balcony before I can invite them in and kneel before me, their lips pursed, awaiting their official duties impatiently. Tired, I give them my hand.

"Now what?" I say, unsure if I'm awake or dreaming, lucid or hallucinating.

"Your eminence, the time has come to move to another location. We've been informed that it's no longer safe here for you. You must come at once."

"At this hour? Where are we going?" I can hear my voice, but the words don't sound as if they're coming from my mouth.

"We're not authorized to speak at this time. We must move quickly. This entire facility is being vacated. The building is under attack."

"Attack? It's the British. I guarantee you, it's Pressinger. When she came to visit, she must've planted a homing device, so they could find me." I'm shivering with excitement. "They want Vadim dead," I practically shout.

Feeling that I have little choice but to comply, I wrap myself in a blanket and leave the gallery for the first time since I arrived. Once we pass through the double doors into the wide hall, they gently take hold of my forearms, and my heart beats faster.

"I really need to rest," I confide. "I don't feel well."

"We'll guide you," one says, though it's too dark for me to make out which one. "There now, we're almost at the end."

I'm not sure what he means by that. It sounds too coddling. But I say nothing, because I can't see where I'm going at all and I don't want my voice to betray any fear. At their nudging, we take a turn and walk down another long hall that has tall windows along one side. From here, I can see the moon, which gives off a pale blue light to work with. Outside, I hear a wheezing, clicking sound, the silhouettes of bobbing heads.

"The British left their kangaroos here," I remark, just to say anything at all. "I used to come here as a child. That was so long ago, but I remember it well. I remember everything."

Neither guard responds.

We arrive at the end of the hall.

"Where are we?"

"We have to leave through an exit in the cellar."

At this point, events get a little hectic and confusing. All I remember is that, as one of the guards opens the door, the second grows aggressive with me, twisting my arm behind my back and then wrapping his arm around my neck. As a seasoned wrestler, I know exactly what I have to do to escape this simple hold, but as a malnourished old man, I fail to thrust the much younger guard over my shoulder. I get so confused sometimes. There are too many days locked inside my head to keep organized. That missed moment costs me everything. The second guard manages to get hold of my legs. We scuffle in the pitch black for a time, a long time, I can't really get a hold of anyone's shirt or sleeve, at times it goes on for so long that I begin to question if I'm not wrestling myself, if I haven't been grappling with my demons this whole time. They throw me down a long and winding staircase. I tumble and tumble without hitting bottom for what seems like an eternity. After a while, it feels like I'm tumbling back down the very steps I've spent my entire life climbing. I don't remember anything beyond that.

Mustafa Bleed Found Dead

Arrests sought for New Nationalists leadership

An early-morning raid against a Lezer terrorist cell has resulted in the discovery of ex-president Mustafa Bleed's body. The development comes after investigators were able to extract new details from one of the militants arrested the day the ex-president was first taken hostage on route to parliament.

The confession set into motion a large-scale operation deep in the Allegory Mountains. Information pointed to a long-abandoned compound known as the British Retreat, which was being used as a base by Lezer extremists, who were reportedly collaborating with foreign agents.

Government forces arriving at the remote mountain compound were met with strong resistance. Elite units fought the terrorists for several hours before they were able to enter the compound. Once inside, they combed the large estate room by room, eliminating any resistance they encountered. Twenty-six militants were killed, and another 13 were taken into custody.

At approximately 5 a.m., soldiers discovered a room containing some of Mustafa Bleed's personal belongings. A search of the entire compound and surrounding forests followed. The former president's body was discovered in a cellar. An onsite medical examination confirmed that he had been tortured. Doctors report that Mr. Bleed suffered significant brain hemorrhaging.

President Vadim Bleed, who has remained out of the country since the election, is expected to return within the next 48 hours to address the nation. A spokesman for his office said the president "is deeply saddened by the fate that has befallen his father and mentor, one of our founding fathers."

At a press conference, Minister of the Interior Constantin Benini revealed new findings that connect opposition leaders Dabny Bolshoi and Lezer parliamentarian Fatma Gavras to the kidnapping of Mustafa Bleed.

He presented a complex web of arm's length militias, for-hire criminal organizations, and foreign spies connecting the Lezer terrorist cell back to the New Nationalists Party. The evidence underlines a troubling international conspiracy to thwart the recent election and compromise our sovereignty.

According to the 47-page report that government officials have made public, problems began in 2010 with an increase in tariffs and operating fees levied retroactively by the Bleed government on all foreign mining entities. The levy was the brainchild of Mustafa Bleed, who used his role as his son's advisor to push through the initiative.

Headwinds were significant. The Americans threatened economic sanctions for fabricated human-rights abuses. At the United Nations, the British government threatened to pull its international aid. The New Nationalists Party accused the government of blackmailing foreign investment in a country that had little leverage.

The report describes a communication network between all four parties deciding on an agitation campaign designed to destabilize the Bleed government. The evidence outlines an intricate network of CIA spies who have infiltrated the country through the uranium companies and wormed their way into New Nationalists.

Lezer parliamentarian Fatma Gavras is singled out as the main agent of communication between the American spy network and the New Nationalists leadership. The militia that kidnapped Mustafa Bleed is a sleeper cell of ethnic Lezers activated by the CIA in the wake of the election.

Tonight, Berloff Gavras and Janusz Gavras, an uncle and a cousin respectively of Fatma Gavras, are in custody for their roles in communicating with the Lezer militia. Both have issued confessions. Fatma Gavras and Dabny Bolshoi have both gone into hiding, and are to be considered enemies of the state.

Given the internal chaos of the New Nationalists Party, President Vadim Bleed has agreed to continue to lead the nation until another election can be called. "When that will be, no one can say," his office admitted.

Vadim Bleed

ANOTHER EUROPEAN ESCAPE has come to an abrupt end. I've stuffed myself back into the starched shirt, stodgy grey suit, boring underwear, and unshapely loafers that citizens expect to see on their presidents, boarded a waiting helicopter on the roof of the Marriott, and flown to the nearest airport. From here I'm expected to take a military plane to Greece, where my staff and private jet await me. Along the way, I'm to be conditioned back into fighting form, quizzed upon the government's talking points and pre-approved answers, and briefed upon every last development that's taken place in my absence. I'm to sit through endless conference calls with ministers, through military strategies meant to defile the opposition, and plead with CEOs to dig their uranium pits ever deeper into our land.

In Thessaloniki, I waited for my private jet to be readied and received a lecture from British ambassador Louise Pressinger, who only ever spoke to me on behalf of the Americans.

"I don't know where to begin," she said as soon as she was on the line. "Normally I don't like to get in the middle of family affairs, but your timing in this particular case, well, it's destabilized the region. It's proven as difficult to manage as you are."

"That's the nature of chaos management. It can pull the carpet out from under everyone's feet."

"Including yours," she said.

"And yet I'm here."

"Now I understand that this distracts people from the election, which is what you wanted. And that's clever. I'll give you credit there. But, and this is a big 'but,' this kidnapping has led to other kidnappings, which have led to murders, which have reignited the kind of tensions that are best kept under lock and key. Everywhere people are angry, at you, at us, at each other. So now it's about Lezers versus Borans, about righting historical wrongs. When you kidnap an ex-president, Vadim, what do you think your enemies see? Don't you think they only see a vulnerable elite who can't protect its own? No one is going to spend one dirty dollar in the middle of this mess."

"We're all aware that this election has gone off the tracks, but maybe that's your fault," I said. "Now we're going to put things right ourselves."

"Alright then. Say you can still walk away with the presidency. At least stop fooling around and forget your father's demands for more tariffs on the uranium mines."

I've won, I thought as I listened to her list the Americans' complaints. I imagined my grandfather looking down on me proudly for what I'd managed. After this, no one will ever doubt me again.

I spent the next half-hour on a call with the General, who took me through the details of the speech I was to give upon my return.

"For security, we'll have the area cordoned off, and everyone who enters the premises will be searched," he assured me. "All

158

surrounding buildings will be secured. We'll have closed-circuit surveillance."

"Wouldn't it be less of a headache for everyone if I delivered a televised speech?"

"People need to see that you're not afraid. Taking back your family's square from the protesters will send the right message. I must inform you that our intelligence network has located your father. He's not going to make it. Use this moment to transform yourself into the country's voice, their way of talking with the man who has affected us all so greatly. Dabny Bolshoi will be charged with murder."

"That's a serious offence," I said. "We should execute him in public, set an example."

"Him and Ms. Gavras. You've been deeply wounded, Mr. President. It's been a dark time, so much like 1983. But the future looks brighter."

We hung up. Even though I was still in Europe, I couldn't help but marvel at how far away my time abroad already felt. As I watch my private jet roll across the runway to the loading station, I can't help but think that, despite the risk, it had been a good move to sneak away, enlist the help of outsiders. Louise Pressinger was just upset because she hadn't secured the Bolshoi win she's worked so hard to organize.

It was messy, yes, but now I'm looking forward. No regrets. Well, actually, I do regret that my Conflict Management lectures are coming up blank in terms of how to best take advantage of all this chaos I've created. What are the ways in which it can all be put neatly back in its box? It irks me that the President of Uganda and the Security Chief of Burma, both of whom attended that class the same semester as me, who opportunistically profited from my absences by selling me their notes before the final exam, neglected to make more mention of the information I so needed at the moment. I'm almost positive that the subsequent lectures on chaos management would've covered those points. Just thinking about that morsel of missing knowledge that could've been nestled comfortably in my head right now, instead of out there lost in the world, makes me want to slap the fun-loving playboy I used to be. If I were to go back, I'd think twice before dropping all my responsibilities the moment the clouds parted in dreary London. All to rent a yacht for a three-day boat party on the Thames. It was so much fun at the time. The weather in London is rarely, if ever, nice. When you're young and the sun is out, you make the most of it.

Transfusion Blog's Kaarina Faasol Missing

by Fatma Gavras

Readers of this necessary space, it falls upon me to inform you that Kaarina Faasol, the brave journalist who published her work here and revealed the Bleeds' atrocities to so many readers beyond our borders, has gone missing. Almost certainly she has been taken by Bleed government forces. Her disappearance comes as a shock but not a surprise. She was acutely aware of the consequences of her actions, and we had planned how to proceed when such an event happened. Well, tragically, here we are.

At around 5 a.m. this morning, Faasol left a message on my answering machine. She said someone was trying to break into her apartment. Then she left the receiver off the hook. What follows is all there, recorded. She had planned that part too. She did not want the Bleeds to make her disappear on their own terms. Faasol has never been one to shy away from danger.

She has never been one to sit comfortably within her relatively protected Boran status. Every word she wrote was infused with that burden of responsibility. There are Borans in this country who disagree with the inequities faced by Lezers, but who draw a line between their lives and the actions of their ruling class. It was never enough for Faasol to live with that privilege. She holds herself to a higher standard, and those of us informed by her work are better for it.

In her nearly two decades as journalist, she went from a novice reporter for our national newspaper, *The Nation*, to one of its editors. In 1997, she began using an alias to publish articles abroad, in the *International Tribune*, where she was first to write about Mustafa Bleed's widespread intimidation of judges, six of whom were murdered for agreeing to hear cases concerning the government seizure of Lezer ancestral lands for mining exploitation.

In 2007, again in the *Tribune*, Faasol broke the story that Mustafa Bleed had suffered a stroke. The coverage upset many people and got her fired at *The Nation*, with the government outright denying the claims. The accusations were never independently confirmed, but Mustafa Bleed was rarely seen in public from that point on. He retired the following year, ceding the presidency to his son Vadim. Faasol appeared to recoil from public view too. In reality, she was imprisoned for three years.

But in recent months, she has commented extensively on the inner workings of our political life through this blog. Her stories often reverberated far beyond our borders to sympathizers around the world, where her reputation remained strong well after she stopped writing. I know this to be true because I regularly enter into conversations with international supporters whose sole point of reference is Faasol's documentation. To the outside world, unmolested by the grotesque contortions of *The Nation*, her perspective on these troubled times is what people know. Whatever happens now, those words are her legacy.

For the moment, she's missing. The police are doing what they can to ensure the case receives as little attention as possible. Nada Ferber, who worked closely with Faasol behind the scenes, has not benefitted from her passport's guarantee of immunity. She has been deported, her newsroom shut down. In the meantime, the Ministry of Information has conveniently continued to operate *The Nation* without any journalists, as a mouthpiece for the Ministry of the Interior. In fact, they have just used its pages to frame me for Mustafa Bleed's death.

You may ask, at this point, what matters anymore if a newspaper can be written entirely by the propagandists who've deported its editors and kidnapped their critics? That we've arrived at this new low showcases the level of desperation within the Bleed government. Their prospects grow dimmer by the day. They are, in effect, pulling out all the stops. We are amidst the bloody last gasps of a dying dynasty that would rather destroy everything than lose control. If we are to pry this nation from the hands of its oppressors, we must be prepared to fight to the end. This is why I will continue to fight for what my dear friend Kaarina Faasol believes in, and for what is inherently good in our nation.

Vadim Bleed

THE STREET POSTERS ARE READY to be pasted across shop windows, and arrest warrants have been issued for any and all NNP operatives out there. It's refreshing to be back on my own jet after all that time in the wild. Once we'd left the runway at Thessaloniki, I started to fiddle with the plane's hi-fi system, and in no time we had bygone balkanized disco anthems wafting through the cabin speakers. I feel good, better than I have in months. That sickly feeling of dire expectation is gone. We are on route to my coronation. Don't you think that, for all the effort we've put into winning this thing, we deserve an in-flight party? Flights can be so boring.

I'm feeling so good that I've just danced through the cabin with an ice bucket and a bottle of vodka in hand, mixing drinks for all my staff. They set down their facade of work (why must they always have their heads buried in papers every time I walk past?) and tentatively began applauding me as I trotted along to the hi-fi's infectious groove. I've worked hard on my speech. I'm positive it's going to be a cathartic fusion of words and ideas, both for me and for the tens of thousands I'm fully expecting to be chanting my name by its end. I'm ready to step out on that stage and bring them all under my wing. My only hope is that I can deliver its volcanic sentimentality with the brute modesty and conditional gravitas that it deserves.

So as I throw fuel on the fire of this party that's beginning to burn out of control around me, I'm also beginning to think in earnest about my second term. There's much to do after my victory speech. I'm approaching 40 – it doesn't show at all, but the time is ripe to grow a beard, imbue my image with some degree of seriousness. The rambunctious playboy is so first term, so junior. With no Pa in the picture, I have to be my own man, the one and only Bleed. What I'd just experienced, this business of running away from my responsibilities, will soon be remembered as the end of a tangential chapter, the final gasps of a lost weekend.

We'd been in the air an hour when I looked out my window, longing to imagine the future against a pristine backdrop. Instead there's the arrow tip of a fighter jet flying alongside us.

"What's that doing there?" I asked a passing stewardess.

"I have no idea," she said, peering over my shoulder. "Why don't I go ask the pilot."

She walked down the cabin to the cockpit, as my eyes remained set on that plane, which in all my travels I'd never once seen outside my window before. What was it doing there now? The stewardess returned. Together, we stared out the window again. It was as if the fighter jet hadn't moved at all.

"The pilot has been in communication with it," she said.

"And?"

"He says it's an escort. We're being diverted from Qala Phratteh's airport. Something to do with a credible threat."

"So where are we going?"

"Kefken Island, about two kilometres offshore Russia."

"The tax haven in the Black Sea? There's nothing there but prisons and mafia runners. What the hell are we going to do there?"

"I'm afraid I don't know, sir."

I looked out the window again and tried to focus. The fighter jet was still there, if a bit blurry at the edges. "Get me the General on the line."

While I waited to be handed a phone with the General on its other end, I surveyed the cabin, which had devolved into a debauched haze of cigar smoking, sports talk, and sweaty cocaine snorting, and wondered whether to turn down the music. It's true that I'd assembled this campaign team with their fortuitous abilities to dive aggressively into party mode as a priority, but at times like this it was a little distracting. It was quite difficult to hear myself think, and when I looked at my hands I saw that I was sweating a fair bit too. I didn't want to frighten anyone, least of all myself. That was probably not the kind of chaos I wanted to invite into this situation. But I may have also been feeling overly self-conscious on account of the drinks I'd had. So I walked around the cabin, telling jokes, patting backs, sampling the lines of cocaine on offer. Things like that don't faze me when my mind is set to work. I simply perk up.

My head shot up from one final line and my nostrils flared with fire. It may have hit me a bit harder than expected. Or maybe the worrisome nature of the current situation had something to do with it. Every time I looked, that fighter jet was still ominously there. Involuntarily I began to dance. By the time the stewardess returned with the phone, a fierce energy had overtaken my body. I gripped the tiny phone with deep resolve and locked myself in the tiny washroom to concentrate.

"What's going on down there? We have a jet escorting us to Kefken Island."

"Things are not good," the General replied.

"Tell me."

"There've been some developments that have complicated the situation."

"Stop shadow-boxing and for fuck's sake get specific."

"Well, it turns out one of your militia kidnapped a journalist."

"And?"

"American intelligence had the journalist under surveillance to begin with. There was a lot of talk about you. Even a conversation where you give what can be interpreted as an order for the kidnapping. It's all been recorded. They're building a case."

"Deny it." I pressed my knuckles into my eyebrows. I remembered a phone call. But I couldn't remember exactly what was said.

"If that were it, we might still be able to contain this. The United Nations, at the request of Norway, is looking into charging you with war crimes for what happened at Revolution Square."

"What happened at Revolution Square for fuck's sake?"

"Things got out of hand. They're accusing you of using chemicals on civilians. If they file these charges in the next hours, they would be able to issue an international arrest warrant for you. So the Americans are pushing to stall your plane."

"What do the Americans want? Land leases, better percentages? Give it to them, whatever it is. Make this go away."

"They want you, Vadim. They want to issue a warrant for your arrest."

I thought again of the fighter jet outside the window. "And you're all too happy to comply."

"I have no choice. You're outside our borders."

I slipped down onto the small toilet. "It all seems so… bleak."

"This is what chaos brings, Vadim. This is why we don't set off into the unknown without a specific idea of where we're going."

"Let's shelve the lecture for the moment."

"We're working on this. We need time. I'm sure we can come up with a deal to get you home."

"What am I supposed to do until then?"

"Whatever you do, don't get off that plane."

International Tribune

Embattled Opposition Figure Arrives in UK, Sheds New Light on Horrors in Mahbad

By NADA FERBER

Special to the International Tribune

Fatma Gavras, an opposition leader who was facing threats to her life in Mahbad, arrived in London yesterday. She was escorted aboard a private plane for British diplomats, who are working to diffuse a deadly impasse. Recent elections have spiralled into widespread chaos and brought the Republic to the brink of civil war.

A doctor drawn into politics by the injustices of her nation's dictatorship, Gavras arrives with little more than the clothes on her back. She has been charged with treason and was the subject of government-sponsored attacks at home.

"We are at a point of no return," Gavras said at a press conference this morning. "This dictatorship has killed too many innocent people in their attempts to rig this election. We can't go back to the way life was before."

Gavras was, by her own estimate, hours away from inevitable arrest or assassination. Dabny Bolshoi, her party's leader on the election ballot, has already been arrested and will almost certainly face execution.

Appearing visibly shaken, Gavras stated that if the world doesn't start paying attention to the Bleeds' growing list of atrocities, all opposition will be slaughtered. The country also risks another genocide of its ethnic Lezer community, as was the case after a contested election led to a civil war in the '80s.

The present situation, according to Ms. Gavras, is untenable. "In the last five years, police service has devolved to a situation where we pay bribes to not be harassed by the police," she claims.

"If you have a shop, a business, if you don't want to be beaten when they randomly pull over your car, if you don't want to risk the rape of a wife or daughter when they bang on your door in the middle of the night, then you have to be ready to pay at any time. It has gotten so bad that the average person has to forego basic necessities in order to keep enough cash on hand for the police."

There has also been a sharp spike in the number of kidnappings in the country over the past five years. According to Gavras, the vast majority of those who disappear are Lezers, opposition members, their relatives, and government functionaries who cross paths with the military.

"The kidnappings have become quite systematic," she says. "Thousands of people gone missing, all disappearing during the daytime, on their way to work or home. No warning and no demands. But once the military gets what it wants from you, all without telling you what it wants, then a body will turn up somewhere on the side of a highway or floating along a river in the cap-ital for all to see. And that's how you learn that the ordeal is over, and that the military is done with you."

Fatma Gavras is the first significant Lezer opposition leader to emerge from the country's political system since the 1980s civil war, which saw over 26,000 Lezers murdered.

Louise Pressinger, Great Britain's ambassador to the region, thinks Ms. Gavras is the right person to lead a government in the event Vadim Bleed should fall. "She has all the ingredients to unite people after what has happened, during their transition toward democratic rule."

Gavras points out that she could just as equally be dead next week. Though she and her family are exiled in London for the time being, she still worries that the long arms of the Bleed intelligence network will catch up with her.

Fatma Gavras may walk away the leader of her homeland, or she may just end up homeless.

Vadim Bleed

OH GOD, IS IT HOT in this plane! We've entered the eighth hour of our standoff on this runway with the cavalry of black Mercedes parked outside, each with its own diplomatic flag, and the afternoon sun is cooking us. It's worse than a sauna in here. Even with my suit gone, I'm basting in my own sweat. The half-nudes surrounding me wouldn't be a problem if not for the fact that somebody in here smells like they romped around in a pool of diced onions before boarding. Of course I'm joking, trying to keep a stressful situation on the lighter side. I know fear when I smell it, and no amount of spritzing the air is going to clear it up.

"I don't feel well," complained the stewardess. "There must be a window somewhere we can open."

"There's no such window on this type of plane," someone replied.

I stood up and surveyed the mess I'd been trying to avoid. Staffers had settled in heaps on the floor of the humid cabin, with clothes strewn on the seats and empty liquor bottles over-flowing from the garbage bin. I decided to say a few words. Not the prepared speech that I was scheduled to give tomorrow as the pinnacle of my political career, but an off-the-cuff contingency speech for today. How I could find myself so close to one outcome and yet so deeply mired in its complete opposite, I didn't know.

"It's obvious to everyone that somewhere along the way we've taken a detour," I said. "Sure, there's the detour that the fighter jet has forced us to make, but as I sit here, I can't help but wonder where along the way we made a more fundamental detour for the leader of our country to end up in this kind of mess. Who's allowed the kind of faulty, short-term thinking that made this once-impossible situation our reality today?"

Everyone looked away, not wanting to confront the obvious.

"It's my father," I continued. When no one denied it, I added, "We're at a crossroads between the old regime and the new regime. We must think past this moment here today, this messy, unpredictable set of events, and consider the long view. They can't hold a sovereign leader. Their efforts are psychological. They want a deal on uranium, as they always have."

A few people sighed and one guffawed.

"You there," I immediately pointed to the source of exasperation. I forget his name. He has such a recognizable face, but one of those endlessly forgettable names. "What's the problem?"

He looked around at the others, as if awaiting their consensus to speak.

"Don't look at them. I'm your president. Talk to me," I said.

"Mr. President," he said, hesitating, "You speak of an error in short-term thinking, but several of us feel that even that is too generous an assessment for what's been going on. There's, how can I say this…"

"Go on." I leaned forward. "Say it."

He looked out the window at the tarmac busy with diplomats and military personnel, and rolled his eyes. "Mr. President, this administration has done no thinking at all. Ever since the election, we've had our heads in the sand as problems cropped up around us. We haven't even been reacting to put out fires. In some cases, we've gone out of our way to make matters worse. The only time we've done anything is to create new problems to distract from the old ones. Your father at least kept control over every detail. He would have foreseen this."

Someone else spoke up now. "Mr. President, what's it worth now? Where are we going from here? We either starve in this plane or go to prison."

"You're wrong," I shouted. "And once we're through here, you're fired. Do you think the General is about to lose his kingpin? Do you think London will give up on 50 years of investment in the Bleeds, today of all days? They were there with us when we founded our nation."

"It's over, Mr. President," a third one conceded. "No one here wants to say it, but I'll tell you the truth: they've conspired against you. There was a chance right after the election that the outcome could have still broken your way, but once you disappeared and your father was kidnapped, the international community lost all faith in this government's ability to manoeuvre. You haven't been involved for months. It's impossible to schedule any kind of meeting with your office."

"I don't believe in the old-fashioned office. I'm a figurehead, a role model. My job is to sell our wares to the world, to bring in the business and big money that create the jobs you sort out. I'm not a bureaucrat. I'm not going to get dragged down into the petty details of your job because, if I did it for you, I'd have to do it for him and him and him and her. I'd become a micromanager, I'd become my father."

"At least your father took charge," someone blurted. "He had plans and he executed them. Things got done."

Finally, my Minister of National Allegiance, a relic from my father's administration who I'd shuffled out of an agriculture portfolio and into overseeing referees and regulations for our recreational handball leagues, spoke up. "You don't set the right example, Vadim. People don't take you seriously."

"Out," I snapped. "Go on. You're out of the caucus for next term. Don't bother showing up to the speech tomorrow night. Go sit in the back of a prisoners' van."

He stood without complaint and said, "It has been an honour serving the Bleeds. Good luck to you all."

The minister collected his briefcase and then fashioned a flag out of a white shirt to signal his surrender. He waited by the door for the stewardess to let him go. The door opened and the stairs swung down, letting in a flood of fresh air.

"Can we leave this open for a short while?" the stewardess asked after the minister had left. "I have asthma, and it's starting to act up."

"You go too," I said.

"Thank you, Mr. President," she said, packing up her belongings in a hurry, as if I would change my mind at any moment. "I have a family, and I'm not really a political person, so if you don't mind my saying so, this doesn't involve me."

"Please feel free to bill us for your overtime," I offered.

"You're too kind," she replied as she backed down the steep staircase.

By then, those left in the cabin were peering out the window to see what had happened to the Minister of National Allegiance. Contrary to what I'd predicted, he wasn't being handcuffed, strip-searched, or shoved into the back of a police van. Instead, he was having a cigarette with some other officials. It looked like they were laughing. Someone brought the minister a bottle of water.

"He's defecting," someone said.

"He was a spy all along," I lied, not sure that I was lying all that much. "We've been feeding him false information to throw off intelligence."

There were five of us remaining on the executive jet, not counting the pilot who we hadn't seen since the landing. He had to stay with the plane under all circumstances, so I assumed he'd barred himself in the cockpit with what little air conditioning was left in reserve and was keeping busy in ways I won't question. So we sat there in silence as the afternoon wore on, doing our best to save energy while the sun beat down and turned the plane into an oven. The only food left were packets of airline peanuts, which we tried to conserve. We had no idea how much longer we would be on the plane.

"I have a victory speech that I will deliver tomorrow if it's the last thing I do," I said. "We just need to buy some time until the General pulls the right strings."

"Do you really think the General has your best interests at heart?" someone said. "Maybe we should just negotiate for ourselves."

"Of course the General has the Bleeds' best interests at heart. Who do you think covers for his every move? We're here because he killed too many people at a demonstration. Do you really think he's going to trust someone else to cover for him like that? Do you think the British are about to trust someone else with everything we've got underway here after 50 years? They all want the Bleeds to stay right where they are. Everyone's better off with the devil they know."

"Can you call the General? Perhaps he can give us a sense of what's going on out there."

"All right. If that's what it takes to keep you on board, then let's get him on the line." I tried the General several times. "If we're stuck here," I turned around to address the ashen-faced staffers who'd been watching my every move, "then I'm sure all hell has broken out where he is."

They all looked at each other, as if strategizing what to do next.

"It's getting late," one said. "I think we've run out of time."

Briefly, I considered executing someone for the sake of morale, but given the cramped confines of this cabin I decided that might do more harm than good. I've also never liked guns.

"You've been good to me, I know," I said, sensing the tide was turning against me. "It's me they want. You're just in the wrong place at the wrong time. If you leave now, I don't know what will happen to you. But I know all this is happening because of me. So whatever you want to do, I'm letting you decide."

"I'm just wondering if we could do more good out there than in here, Mr. President," one of them said, I'm not sure who. I was no longer paying attention to any of them all that much. "Someone should be out there speaking on your behalf, don't you think?"

"You might be right," I said. It was getting late, and the sun was beginning to go down. Outside, the shadows of the plane and cars stretched across the tarmac. "You can all go. I'm going to stay here."

"Do you want us to request anything for you? Food or water? Some bedding?"

"I'll be all right. I'm a Bleed."

"You are, sir." They all bowed. "It's been an honour serving you."

"I sincerely hope to see you all tomorrow night at Revolution Square."

"Wouldn't miss it for the world, Mr. President."

"It's going to be a great celebration. Trust me, we'll be laughing about this mess in 24 hours' time."

They began to applaud as if it were already the next evening, but didn't have the energy to sustain it for long.

"Go on, get some fresh air."

I stood at the door to give them each a firm hug as they lined up with white shirts in hand, ready to walk down. They were good staffers. One by one they left, shooting up their hands as quickly as possible so that the waiting soldiers wouldn't shoot. They managed a few steps before they were tackled down and frisked. Unlike the minister, they were handcuffed right away.

I closed the plane's door behind me. There was nowhere to go and nothing to do. In the distance, the sun was touching the horizon and everything was bathed in an orange light. I expected that the soldiers would finally receive the order to ambush the plane sometime after dark, whatever the risks. Their commanders would find a way to fabricate the story they wanted to tell once morning came. It was over. I had my victory speech in hand, but nowhere to give it. I sat there, on the carpeting, the coolest part of the cabin, for what felt like hours, brooding. I had a pretty good idea of what would happen to figureheads like me once our supporters tired of putting us on show. The pendulum swings, the world wants to feel good again about pushing us out front, using our cover to get their work done. We're hauled before the courts, scolded for all that was done on our watch, run through a list of the victims they'd killed in our names, trampled unjustly so that the next man in line can have a strong platform upon which to voice a message of justice, hope, and change. I have that speech in my pocket! But no one thinks I'm the right man to give it. How utterly depressing.

As night settled in, the choices available in the next few hours of my life grew painfully clear. I was just about to surrender, get on with it and leave the plane, when, to my surprise, the door opened and the General stepped in.

International Tribune

Mahbad Dictator Vadim Bleed Negotiating Exit

By NADA FERBER

Special to the International Tribune

An unexpected standoff on a remote Russian island outpost in the Black Sea could bring an end to 50 years and three generations of single-family rule in Mahbad. President Vadim Bleed is holed up in his private plane on a runway, where American fighter jets escorted him as he tried to re-enter Mahbad's airspace.

Officials close to the situation are reporting that the beleaguered dictator is prepared to negotiate an exit strategy that could pave the way for new leadership. This fast-moving development is a matter of events falling into place at just the right time, according to officials.

"We could not have planned or coordinated any of this," said Louise Pressinger, British ambassador to the region. "But now that it's happening, we're prepared to use any and all leverage available to us to produce a once-in-a-lifetime change in the region."

Ms. Pressinger is working alongside delegations from Norway, the United States and the United Kingdom. Speaking in the United Nations Security Council, Russian and Chinese delegates have both insisted that they approve any agreement made between the parties. "Given the geopolitical landscape that this sort of change in leadership may bring about, everyone wants to ensure that their concerns are met," said one official who spoke on condition of anonymity.

Asked if Russia or China might offer Vadim Bleed exile in exchange for amnesty, the official refused comment. "There's a portfolio of priorities on every table, and a lot of tables. In the end, a deal will depend on how many of those priorities can be met."

Pressinger has reported that negotiations have already resulted in the release of numerous Bleed officials and a stewardess from the plane. "Mr. Bleed, we are told, appears dejected and cornered. He knows a cul-de-sac when he sees one. Given the circumstances, it may just be a matter of time."

Bleed finds himself diplomatically stranded on foreign soil with only a tenuous grasp on his presidency. The British, who have long represented their former colony on the international stage, are at a loss as to how to defend his recent massacre of Lezers at an anti-government demonstration. They appear to have invested their faith in recently exiled opposition leader Fatma Gavras after the unlawful arrest of the New Nationalists Party presidential candidate Dabny Bolshoi.

News of what may be Bleed's last stand has sent shock waves across his home country. Scores of military personnel have begun to abandon their posts. According to local reports, citizens are flocking into the streets at the news that their dictator may be stepping down. Celebrations erupted at Revolution Square, the flashpoint for so many of this election cycle's battles, calling for a new era.

The Ministry of the Interior, said to be more loyal to former president Mustafa Bleed than to his son, has largely let the demonstrations grow unchecked. On the day that Vadim Bleed was supposed to deliver a victory speech, the square was instead filled with thousands of the people his government had tried to oppress.

Vadim Bleed

"WHAT'S HAPPENED HERE?" the General gestured with gloved hands as he surveyed the mess that had befallen the cabin.

"I let the help go," I replied somewhat despondently. "To what good fortune do I owe this visit? I thought you weren't taking my calls."

"Phones are sensitive. I did see you were calling. It's better that we speak in person now, don't you think?"

"You're here to lure me off the plane. You've never been on my side, I know. You'd sooner work for them. A foil."

"I'm working *with* them, Vadim. I work *with* everybody. For the country's benefit. As always. Everyone wants the most beneficial outcome. Times have changed. What worked a generation ago no longer goes unquestioned today. We gave it a good try."

"So what's been decided out there? The strongman is out of fashion. If that's how it's going to be, I'd sooner step off this plane and concede the election. Resign. Walk away. That's still an option, I'm sure."

"If you step out, the only thing that will happen is you'll be arrested. Then you'll be smeared all over the world and you'll be blamed for things you never knew you did but that were done by someone, somewhere, in your name. You'll be put on trial, your family's legacy will be dismantled, you'll spend the rest of your life in a cell as historians tarnish and scrub you out of the nation's history, and if you don't die by execution, you'll die of poor health and indignity."

"Sounds like you've planned it all out."

"Or we can fly away. Right now."

"And go where?"

"Disappear. Exile. The terms of which can't be formally negotiated until we are up in the air. But the groundwork for such a last-case scenario, I can tell you, has been in place ever since your father's time."

"My father," I said glumly. "Here he is again, making plans for me right up until the very end."

"Shall we?" He pointed up.

I waved him off as if to say get on with it, the choice is obvious. Then I asked the all-important question. "What happens to my money?"

The General delivered an intricate knock on the door to the cockpit. "A big chunk of it will unfortunately disappear as the price of doing business. But, you know, there's been enough stowed away over the years, away from the banks, so that you won't have to worry for many years."

I felt the plane rock gently as the engines whirred back to life. The air conditioning was restored, and soon it was cool enough to put on my shirt again. The plane began to move, and we watched the show outside as everyone pretended to be caught off guard. They trotted alongside the pilot's window, waving him to stop. But he didn't and soon they were running next to us. Then we left them behind, and I could see the last soldier fulfilling his duties, running in exasperation and then giving up. The tires left the ground.

Can I tell you how relieved I felt once that decrepit airstrip finally disappeared behind us? Apart from on the racetrack, I've never had such a close call. So once the plane had levelled off and it became evident that we were on our way toward unknown horizons with a comfortable nest egg in tow, I got up and began to do a routine of yogic stretches.

"It's a shame it has to end this way," I complained as I lay on my back, contorting my right leg in an effort to air out my lumbar. "I had a good thing going with the Chinese. They could've helped us modernize. You can't deny this is all happening because we've been in bed with the same people for way too long."

"There are many pieces to every puzzle. You can't always produce the outcome you'd like."

I switched legs and breathed deeply, then exhaled. "Still, these exiles, they can be temporary. I imagine Borans are going to get pretty sick of whoever steps in next. There's a lot of dangerous people who are going to feel put out. It won't be long before nostalgia sets in and people pine for the old days."

"People are funny that way."

"What's going to happen now? You must know."

"I'm afraid the excitement is over for most people. We're going to wrap up the loose ends from this election. We tried to get our people back in the door the old-fashioned way, but it didn't work this time. So now we find a way to move on. You're part of that, just as I am. Louise Pressinger and the Americans want Gavras. They think it will be good for morale to finally have the opposition take charge, a Lezer in leadership. And for the business end of things, managing the mines, she appears to be very accommodating to what the Americans want over the long term. But I don't know that we can work with her. Too much of a progressive in all the wrong ways. I don't know how long I can guarantee her safety in the vacuum of the transition years. So many scars must heal before we find the right order again. Regime change is a messy business. A lot of powerful people are going to be disappointed before anyone is happy again."

I pushed off the ground into a back-bridge. "I still don't understand how you can't see what the Chinese are offering. We're a small country that needs assurances. We don't benefit from declaring allegiance to just one superpower and leaving it at that. We have to create competition and get the best deal for our uranium in an ever-changing world. To think what we could have done with those extra revenues."

"Maybe your friends the Russians and Chinese can't be trusted to deliver. Maybe it would all go poorly in six months' time. Where would we be then?"

"How many American spies are working at those uranium mining offices now? I'd be surprised if anyone who's left there knows how to dig a hole."

"The benefits we get in exchange are guaranteed. The military budget is more generous than any operating tax you can impose. We do as we like, as long as we share certain information. That's our place in the world order: uranium, information, and use of our territory should a larger conflict ever break out with the East. We're aligned, protected. What if the Chinese and Russians are working on deals all over the world just like the one they offered you? Maybe there are three other presidents out there like you, or maybe there are 30. Maybe they expect this to fall through. Maybe they genuinely want the uranium in exchange for new technologies, or maybe they're simply interested in obstructionism. Maybe they're looking over your head at something bigger. Maybe it's more worth their while to spend time and money making it harder for someone else, to make their enemies spend more of everything, to distract attention from more valuable pursuits. Maybe that's their game. Maybe we're just pawns and the most unwise move we can make is to think otherwise. You have to take all these things into consideration when striking up a deal with the shifty kingmakers of another king. It's a world of maybes out there."

"So you think I crossed a line then. You would have been happy if I'd kept racing cars and throwing parties."

"I would have been happy had you kept me in the loop and not run off in the middle of an election cycle when everything is up for grabs. And I would have been able to help you, had you not taken the bait."

"Is that what it was?"

"Context is everything. You can't assume to know the intentions of anyone who's talking to you."

"Whose bait did I take then? The Chinese's or the Americans'? Or maybe it was yours."

"It could have been anyone's and everyone's. In the end, we're all compelled to offer bait every day. But it was you who took it. The responsibility always falls on those who take it."

"It was you."

"I manage national security. We live in a security state, where leadership questions can sometimes be a distraction. I choose between undesirable prospects every day."

"But it's not your job to take responsibility."

"No, not per se. I'm in the business of redistribution. See, despite appearances, we have a healthy history with the Americans and British. They support us in so many ways that aren't obvious on the surface."

"They bankroll you."

"You're too young to remember where it all came from. Our part of the world is so restive, it has been that way from the moment the very idea of an independent nation was born under your grandfather. We'll always be better at being a regional intelligence infrastructure than a nation. We have to put someone out front to play the decision-maker, but when all is said and done, making too many decisions is always bad news for a region like ours. We're not funded for our bold decisions. But we're supported handsomely to accept that. Your father, now there was someone who knew how to strike the right balance between direct nationalist fervour and our more indirect strategic calculations. He was a military man at heart."

"I'm not sure what you expect to happen once all the uranium is dug out of the ground and sold off. I actually wanted to get something done for our people."

"But our people don't want that from you. You're a Bleed. They want the new direction from someone new."

"Well, that's the feel-good thought of the day." I was no longer stretching by then, but sitting across the aisle from him, looking out the window. We were back over the Black Sea, with no land in sight. "So where are you taking me? Malta? The Canary Islands? Fiji? Who's doing the negotiations while we're up here?"

"There's nowhere left to go, Vadim. It's over. You can only disappear. If we resettle you somewhere else, someone will find you. Lezer rebels, CIA, MI5, someone will hunt you down. If there's ever a war-crimes trial like they're threatening, well, everything is at risk. A lot has been done in your name since you've been away. It's the International Criminal Court that's in motion now. Now people want to prosecute the past. If it all goes ahead as planned, it risks the status of our donors and our whole security apparatus. No one wants that."

"I haven't ordered anything. It's not my sword to fall on. They want to prosecute me for my father's war."

"But on paper you have. Everything has happened on paper. If the most recent roundup of Lezers hadn't happened after the election, then you might have a leg to stand on. But it did, it had to because of events you set into motion. And so now your name is tied to a massacre."

"Sounds like entrapment to me. I set nothing into motion. It had to be you. You're behind everything. This is your coup. You had my pa murdered, didn't you? It's all becoming clear now. You made me feel bad about that for a second, but if it was you who baited me with Jojo and the Russians, then it was also you who staged Pa's kidnapping with the Russians and had the Chinese lure me in. You're wiping the slate clean."

"Perception is a complicated thing. It can get so messy. You, my boy, only have one decision left to make. I can inform you that you have only one door left open to you. It's up to you what happens next."

The General stood up, held me firmly by the forearm and led me over to the airplane's door. There, he attached himself to the wall with a security belt, and then pulled the door open. Cold air flooded in, pushing our hair back as we stood there, watching the impenetrable expanse of pre-dawn sky blend into the blue water below, just as first light was beginning to creep in. I've never seen a sunrise so beautiful as that.

With a pistol in his hand, he gestured out the door and waited for me to make up my mind. "Do the noble thing and take care of it yourself," he shouted through the rush of wind storming in. "History will think better of you for it."

International Tribune

Vadim Bleed Steps Down, Ending Dictatorship in Republic of Mahbad

By NADA FERBER

Special to the International Tribune

Facing mounting international pressure to step down, Mahbadian President Vadim Bleed has agreed to go into exile. His refusal to accept election losses two weeks ago fed a popular revolt that mushroomed into a revolution. It has resulted in one of the most serious crises along the Middle Eastern/Transcaucasian fault line in three decades.

The International Red Cross estimates that well over 1,000 people have died as a result, while another 1,500 have gone missing in the surge of sectarian kidnappings that have rocked the country.

Bleed's departure ends 50 years of family rule. In exchange for relinquishing any future family claim to the presidency, Bleed has accepted an offer of political asylum at an undisclosed location.

The deal emerged after an emergency 12-hour negotiation session between Bleed and delegates from the United States, Great Britain, Norway and SUMCAX, the regional trading bloc of uranium-mining countries that leases Kefken Island in the Black Sea from Russia.

"It's not a perfect arrangement, but its historical significance is undeniable," said Britain's ambassador to the region Louise Pressinger, one of the deal's principal architects.

Under the terms of the agreement, Minister of the Interior Constantin Benini emerges as the interim leader until the country is stable enough to hold another election. A longstanding figure within the country's military community, Benini has a strong reputation as a backroom broker with historic ties in the region and beyond.

Pressinger says the West Point graduate was often called upon to substitute for Vadim Bleed at international meetings and even in relations between former president Mustafa Bleed and his son, who were reportedly on bad terms. Mr. Benini is now left with the monumental task of restoring order in the country after weeks of debilitating setbacks.

As news of Vadim Bleed's exile began to circulate among citizens, thousands have converged upon Revolution Square to celebrate. Just days ago, Mr. Bleed was expected to deliver a major speech there to inaugurate his second term.

There were also reports of looting in some neighbourhoods. The police, typically an omnipresent force in the capital of Qala Phratteh, are conspicuously absent from the streets. Though troops are present in the city, they appear to have orders to protect only government buildings and SUMCAX holdings.

It's too early to say just who has the ability to lead the nation after the Bleeds have systematically decimated its institutions for half a century. Dabny Bolshoi, the New Nationalists Party presidential candidate who ran against Vadim Bleed, was recently arrested in conjunction with the kidnapping of Mustafa Bleed. What becomes of him in a post-Bleed scenario remains to be seen.

Pressinger believes that the NNP may have claimed up to 60 per cent of the vote in the recent election. The majority of those votes can be credited to NNP candidate Fatma Gavras, the Lezer parliamentarian in exile who captured the imaginations of many people from all backgrounds.

"She really managed to tap into what most citizens thought was wrong with their nation," Pressinger said. "Af-

ter the Bleeds, people don't want another elite. They want someone in charge who knows their experience."

Just hours before Bolshoi was arrested, Gavras and her family were flown to London. Reached for comment, she said, "The Bleeds leave behind an open wound that will take many years to heal. Much blood has been spilled and this exile deal leaves none of that accounted for."

She would neither confirm nor deny whether she plans to return home and run for president in the eventuality of an election.

Meanwhile, uranium futures jumped today at news of the regime change. The nation, though tiny, is home to one of the largest natural deposits of uranium in the region. New arrangements for the international sales of uranium, Pressinger confirmed, will help the post-Bleed nation rebuild its institutions.

As part of laying the groundwork for the next election, Benini has promised to first set up a public inquiry into how deeply Bleed corruption penetrates the government bureaucracy. "Going forward, I intend to root out all remainders of Bleed corruption and help forge a new government workforce so that, when the time comes for presidential elections, this nation will have a stronger foundation."

Asked how long he envisions that process taking, he noted that it could potentially take a year or more. Though repairing relations with the uranium-mining industry and international partners tops his agenda, there are numerous domestic issues that also require attention.

"Now that we've arrived at this moment of change," Benini noted, "it's impossible to say just how much change must take place. We must talk to our people. So much has been left unattended for so long."

Vadim Bleed

IT'S NOT MY FIRST TIME being pushed out of a plane. But this is my first time without a parachute. I'm facing up toward the universe. I can't be bothered to have the wind beating at my face. I've spread my arms and legs, and I must say that I'm glad to have donned my blazer before making the leap because its tails are fluttering like wings and keeping me afloat all that much longer. I don't have much time. Obviously. But every second in life matters. Have I put up enough of a struggle, you may wonder? Did I simply kowtow to demands all along? Did I try to change course too late? Maybe. Time will tell. They say that beginnings are mysterious, that opening salvos are necessarily but one choice drawn from an infinite number of possibilities. After that, every move you make is a narrowing down of the choices to come. And the end, well, that's just an inevitability. It just so happens you're hurtling through the air at that moment and the great game of musical chairs you play with all your associates and adversaries has come up short for you. I feel rather Zen about the whole thing. I no longer have a choice, do I?

The plane's gone from sight now. For a while I could see it, at first in all its details, with the General standing at the open door as I fell farther away. Then it was the size of a toy. Then it became the tip of a white trail of smoke. And now there's nothing there, just me falling.

I suppose I'd better use this time wisely and pass along some final requests. Can you tell my mother that I'm sorry? She was right. No one character can be larger than his story. I was a Bleed then, and I am a Bleed now. My mistake was to think that I could ever be someone else. But I love her, and I miss her, and that may not be worth much to her, but it's meant some things to me in my 37 years.

Tell my people that, sadly, life's not going to get any better. They, too, have little control over their story, as they'll soon find out. We Bleeds may have appeared to rule over them with an iron fist, but once we're gone they'll quickly learn that my family existed only to give them the false impression that just one man stood between them and the lives they desired. But really, there are so many people who stand between ordinary people and the lives they want to lead. And beyond those people, there are other governments and world machinations and the price of uranium. Tell them they shouldn't have tampered with the stability they once enjoyed in return for the mess they're about to inherit. Social anthropologists, that London School professor who gave me a c once, and other academic types will surely write peer-reviewed essays about the deep wounds of dictatorship on a national psyche. They'll argue how you weren't set up to govern yourselves because you've been abused by governance for so long. But really, it's not true. Bleeds gambled for the best lives we could get for our people, and so what if we put a little aside for ourselves along the way. Look at the consequences we have to contend with.

Tell my pa, if he's still alive, that our public animosity was used against us. Enemies can make people so predictable. I wish I'd learned that sooner. Better off being like the General, friend to everyone. Congrats, Pa, I hope this all worked out as you thought it would. But really, I'm guilty here too. I could have made better choices along the way, then maybe I wouldn't be here now. Chaos management has pulled the rug out from under me in the end. Or maybe I would be here anyways. Perhaps this is some variation of my fate that was written the day I was born.

Tell the world that they're wrong about people like me. Bleeds didn't take anything from anyone. We were put into place as a cheaper alternative to empires. And now these old imperialists have arrived at a point where we're no longer needed because the global economy can reach far enough on its own to not need middlemen like us to grease the wheels of trade anymore. Or because we have our own crazy ideas about how that trade should benefit our people. Here's a thesis for you London Schoolers. We Bleeds, along with all the world's other strongmen, were a stopgap between the age of imperialism and the era of globalization. That would be the paper I would write at this moment. And all that democracy they keep pushing on us is a fail-safe that gives other governments the opportunity to change course on our country's policies if things don't go as they please. Would they give me an A this time? Probably not.

Well, enjoy President Benini or President Gavras or whoever you're going to get. I'm sure it won't be boring. The air's not as thin anymore, and nowhere near as cold. I can see the water below clearly now. Just a moment ago I thought this fall was taking forever. Just goes to show: you scheme and you plan and you wait for the right moment to make your move and then all of sudden – *poof!*

Acknowledgements

This novel could not have been completed without the help of a valuable support network that encircles my writing life. First and foremost, I thank my wife Karolina and my son Luca, for their steadfast belief in what I do. I am immensely grateful to have a friend, mentor, and publisher such as Simon Dardick in my life, and to be able to work with editor Andrew Steinmetz. The shaping of this novel's newspaper articles would not have been possible without the guidance of former *Montreal Gazette* editor Bryan Demchinsky. Both the Canada Council for the Arts and the Conseil des arts du Québec were generous in their financial support during the process of writing this book. Finally, I would like to thank Neil Smith and Andy Sinclair, who read and commented on early versions of this manuscript, and Diane Carlson, who proofed its pages.